W9-BKW-742

On Top of
Spoon Mountain

Also by John Nichols

FICTION

The Sterile Cuckoo
The Wizard of Loneliness
The Milagro Beanfield War
The Magic Journey
A Ghost in the Music
The Nirvana Blues
American Blood
An Elegy for September
Conjugal Bliss
The Voice of the Butterfly
The Empanada Brotherhood

NONFICTION

If Mountains Die (with William Davis)
The Last Beautiful Days of Autumn
On the Mesa
A Fragile Beauty
The Sky's the Limit
Keep It Simple
Dancing on the Stones
An American Child Supreme

On Top of
Spoon Mountain

JOHN NICHOLS

UNIVERSITY OF NEW MEXICO PRESS
Albuquerque

17 16 15 14 13 12   1 2 3 4 5 6

Library of Congress Cataloging-in-Publication Data

Nichols, John Treadwell, 1940–
  On top of Spoon Mountain / John Nichols.
    p. cm.
  ISBN 978-0-8263-5270-5 (cloth : alk. paper) —
  ISBN 978-0-8263-5272-9 (electronic)
  1. Older men—Fiction.
  2. Mountaineering—Fiction. I. Title.
  PS3564.I274O5 2012
  813'.54—dc23

                                    2012012396

Jacket illustration by Rini Templeton

Composed in 11.5/15.5 Warnock Pro
Display type is Caslon Antique

For my granddaughters
Solana, Sierra, and Lucinda.
And for their parents, too.

Also for my pals
Rick Smith and Sean Murphy:
Dos Muchachos en la Biblioteca.
We've scaled heights together, and
even "Wild Horses" can't stop us!

Rewind history, please.
I want another chance.

One

Forty-eight hours after my visit to the emergency room, I decided to climb Spoon Mountain on my sixty-fifth birthday in three weeks. I am not saying that's the smartest idea I ever had in my life, but I've always been a stubborn case. I'm a novelist, I write screenplays, I'm an athlete, I have been married three times, I can live with pain. I wanted to climb that mountain on my birthday with my children, Ben and Miranda. They were not pleased at the prospect.

Ben said, "I don't think you should be climbing mountains right now, Pop. You don't look so hot to me. Spoon Mountain is twelve thousand nine hundred and ninety-nine feet high."

Ben is thirty-eight, he weighs two-ten and measures six-two. He has a square jaw, a crew cut, and hooked to his belt is a Leatherman, a tape measure, and a Verizon cell phone. Ben is a construction worker and he's good at it, as conscientious as the day is long. He takes really good care of his tools. You can trust him to go out of his way to make everything okay. He is a sure bet.

I said, "Ben, I need to show you and Miranda where to scatter my ashes. We'll have fun like in the old days up high.

It will be a gorgeous trip. Maybe we'll see a bighorn sheep. You will remember it forever."

Ben said, "I don't *want* to scatter your ashes, Pop, you're not going to die. Calm down, you're tripping out. How much did you have to drink?"

Then he hung up and called Miranda in the Capital City three hours south, and four seconds later Miranda dialed me to read me a riot act.

"What do you mean you're going to climb Spoon Mountain on your birthday in three weeks? Have you gone completely mental, Dad? Ben says you went to the ER because you thought you were having a heart attack."

"No way." I explained to her carefully, "It was a minor case of indigestion that segued into a teensy panic attack compounded by excruciating abdominal spasms due to gas. In short, I ate something that did not agree with me. A false alarm."

"I don't believe it for a minute," Miranda said. "You always lie about everything. You live in denial."

I said, "I made a promise. I am scared if we don't do it right now we'll never climb that mountain again. The fire danger is mounting. The Feds might close the national forest. Time is running out."

"What do you mean 'we,' Johnny?" she interrupted. "Maybe I'm not tracking this correctly but if my memory serves I believe you have an annuloplasty ring in your mitral valve; you fluctuate in and out of serious atrial fibrillation on a daily basis despite all the Lanoxin and Coumadin you ingest; you can't walk straight because of the oscillopsia; and when was the last asthma attack that floored you—six weeks ago? And that's merely for starters. I feel as if I'm listening to a quadriplegic inform me he's planning to dance the lambada all night with Charo."

I hate it when Miranda calls me "Johnny." She has been doing that as the ultimate put-down since her eighth birthday. My name is Jonathan Kepler, and nobody except Miranda (and my girlfriend, Sally) calls me Johnny. But Sally does it in Spanish which is okay by me. I am not a formality freak, however Jonathan is my first name, not Johnny, or Jack, or Jon. It has always been Jonathan. Of course, over the years I have taken flak about my John Hancock's resemblance to that of the German astronomer Johannes Kepler, who developed Kepler's three laws of motion explaining our planets' elliptical orbits around the sun. When Miranda became aware of the astronomer during her sarcastic teenage years she invented, in her brilliant ignorance, Jonathan Kepler's Three Laws of Motion:

1. My dad is totally elliptical.
2. My dad orbits around heavenly bodies with big boobs.
3. Gravity always pulls my dad in the wrong direction.

Very funny, Miss Smarty Pants.

Two

My girlfriend, Sally Trevino, is almost fifty. She has three teenage boys, Alex, Zachary, and Jason, typical adolescent Neanderthals who believe that *Kill Bill*, a film by Quentin Tarantino, is "awesome." She had them in her thirties. Her ex-husband, Don the Man, despite the restraining order, is probably lurking right now in Sally's garage with an ax, his yuppie Rasta hairdo positively crackling from jealousy. Although they've been divorced eight years Don is one of those Deep South cracker backhoe jockeys who doesn't *get it*. On the Plaza Don once used a public garbage can to bash out the windshield of Sally's Isuzu Trooper. When two cops arrived eager to discourage this erratic behavior, Don performed a full-speed headbutt into their cruiser's front grille and wound up undergoing brain surgery for a subdural hematoma.

Sally has the same kind of mouth as Miranda, except she is the Latina version:

"Híjole! Grow up, nene, are you crazy? Are your children supposed to carry you up that mountain piggyback? Or are you planning to rent a motorized high-altitude wheelchair? I can picture you locked in atrial fibrillation above the timberline facing hurricane-force winds. *You must be out of your mind.*"

"I really need to climb that mountain with my kids," I explained. "I've been a terrible father. We used to revel in nature. I don't want to die without sharing something remarkable and important with them one last time that they can cherish forever. And besides, years ago I made a promise."

Sally is mercurial. She can shift tack on a dime and get eight cents change.

"Querido Juanito," she said, suddenly gentle, placating. "You're a nice human being. I love you. We might even have a future together if you ever see things my way. Don't ruin it, please."

"You don't understand," I said. "I'm nervous. I feel weird. Fire danger is imposing on my window of opportunity. What if the Floresta closes the national forest?"

Sally tilted back and cocked her head, eyeing me. She knows that when I'm the Rock of Gibraltar I cannot be moved. She also knows I'm a failed dad, I'm afraid of all-out commitment to her, I'm a clever though increasingly desperate writer, and I'm probably way more bollixed up healthwise than I admit. So what does she see in me? Well, despite my age I'm fun, I bestow upon her the energy of my infatuation, I make her laugh, and we have good sex thanks to a better life through chemistry. And Sally thinks I may come around because despite *her* age she is still hot stuff. You might say we complement each other.

I could see her gears grinding. Then she leaned forward

and tucked an index finger underneath my chin. The gesture seems affectionate but it's a warning sign.

"I'm on your side," she said. "So if you really want to commit suicide I know an easier way." She kissed me, light as a feather. "Call Don the Man on his cell phone—I'll give you the number—and tell him we screw each other. He will go postal, I promise. We're not talking here about a sentient human being. Don has two assault rifles, a shotgun, eight pairs of Chuck Norris nunchucks, and a can of pepper spray."

Then Sally leaned back again, folding her arms, and smiled at me, saying, "It'll be way more fun for you than dying on a mountaintop."

Three

old on a sec. Let's retreat and come back in again.
For starters, I am *not* suicidal. I am *not* going to
die on a mountaintop. I am *not* an overweight pot-
bellied Marlboro-smoking sexagenarian. This movie is *not*
titled *All That Jazz* and I am *not* Bob Fosse being played by
Roy Scheider. Every cat has nine lives and I have used up
only six of mine. I am still a viable human being and don't
let anyone tell you different.

For the record, I have climbed mountains all my life,
I'm an outdoors type. I ran cross-country in college and
I played postgraduate ice hockey and tennis until health
problems modified my energy level not long ago. I said
modified, that's all. Sure, I'm a trifle worse for wear because
I have been married three times to members of the glamorous intelligentsia, and it is also true I've had a couple dozen
girlfriends between my brief legal liaisons who were not
exactly radical feminists wearing blue jeans and Birken-
stock sandals. No question, that took a toll. I am not proud
of being a sucker for flair over content but that is my problem, nobody else's. You can't cry over spilt milk.

After my first divorce, whenever one of those lady
friends showed up on my doorstep Ben and Miranda dialed

911 or whatever its equivalent used to be. When she was still a kid in Baby Gap OshKosh B'gosh bib overalls Miranda told me she wanted to be a doctor so she could "pronounce" me when I had a heart attack from too much "fooling around." I don't know where she learned the term "pronounce you." But it's not going to happen anytime soon, Miranda, so quit planning your funeral outfit and your mourning wardrobe. I am *not* going anywhere. You can take that to the bank.

As a kid Miranda was a precocious wisenheimer in contrast to taciturn Ben. Extrovert, introvert. Ben is two years older but he seems younger. Back during childhood he liked to get muffled up in his tattered blankets on Sunday nights to watch *Star Trek* reruns. He never spoke a word he was so enthralled by William Shatner and his outer-space buddies. Miranda would perch beside him sipping her hot chocolate with a melted marshmallow on top snidely telling Captain Kirk to wear a jockstrap, Spock that his ears were falling off, and scoffing "Beam me up, Scotty, this is so *lame*" whenever a cyclops with a prehensile forehead appeared on the starship *Enterprise*.

Miranda admits, "Ben reminds me of Al on *Tool Time* in that Tim Allen TV show *Home Improvement*." She won't say that to Ben's face. Miranda loves Ben more than life itself. "If anybody ever messed around with my big brother," she warns even today, "I would hand them the biggest knuckle sandwich in America."

The trouble with Miranda is she's really smart. You can't outthink or out-diagnose her or out-argue her. If you want to discuss Kant or the Transcendentalists she can talk you into a corner and then take away your paintbrush.

If you want to schmooze about Brett Favre and the Green Bay Packers she will run you ragged with statistics and wacko sports opinions. Growing up, Miranda would snuggle beside me watching NFL games on Sundays. We were fans. Sometimes Ben accompanied us and he never paid attention. He would rather fiddle with his Rubik's Cube or study his book on how to make a go-cart or build your own remote-control model airplane. When the Super Bowl came around Ben never even knew (or cared) who was playing. And he never solved, not even once, his Rubik's Cube.

Miranda, on the other hand, would force me to bet real money with her on the game. Like two dollars or five dollars—serious stuff. If my team won I always made a joke stating I hadn't been betting for real, forget about it. This incensed Miranda. She would have none of my magnanimous pity and promptly smashed her piggy bank to fork over the cash. "Here's your money, you son of a bumblebee."

"Don't talk that way," I scolded. "It's not ladylike."

"Don't tell me what to do," she fired back. "I'm not your slave."

If her team won the Super Bowl Miranda's hand was outstretched in my face for the gelt while confetti still fluttered onto the field. "Pay up," she'd gloat. "I want my Maypo."

Ben hated gambling. When we used to play poker for matchsticks at the kitchen table before bedtime he never bought into the program. He did not like the sense of competition. It was emotionally too treacherous. Why couldn't we simply play for fun?

"Because real life isn't for *fun*," Miranda explained when she was only seven or eight years old. "It's a dog-eat-dog world out there, Ben. Some people get the glory, and everybody else gets the poop. Learn to live with it."

She solved his Rubik's Cube the first time she tried it.

Four

A couple of days after Sally took me to task, Miranda left a message on my answering machine:

"Hi, Papa-san, are you still alive? How come my phone isn't ringing with you on the other end? If you don't contact us toot sweet, Michael and me and Lizzy will drive up there in person and kick your booty big time."

Michael is Miranda's husband. Lizzy is their kid. She's seven and a half years old. Michael is a plumber who tends the home office all day long handling calls and cell phoning his crews around the city on emergency jobs. Michael specializes in emergencies twenty-four hours around the clock. The People's Plumber. He makes a lot of money because he's a grown-up businessman with a quarter-page ad in the phone book. I'd call him dependable, brave, clean, courteous, and honest, sort of like Ben only more outgoing. Michael's favorite TV sitcom reruns are *Roseanne* and *That '70s Show*. He has breadth. Ben never watches television.

Lizzy is a mischievous pistol (think Eloise at the Plaza Hotel), the spitting image of Miranda at Lizzy's age. I really love Lizzy and she loves me. She has a big cage in her room inhabited by three happy rats. There's also a Siamese fighting fish in a bowl on the windowsill. His name is Angelina

Aguilera. The rats are called Wynken, Blynken, and Nod. Lizzy is on the jump rope team at her school and she can do fifteen Buttbumps in a row so fast you can't even see the rope. She is very coordinated, which must be a trait inherited from me. Despite some naysayers' opinions I am not all bad. At least I used to think so.

I reached Miranda on the fifth-floor pediatric ICU of University Hospital where she was caretaking a five-year-old girl attached to life support after being wounded by a ricochet from a drive-by shooting. Miranda is thirty-six, and Lizzy starts third grade next fall.

"I worry when you don't call," my daughter said. "How's the old sump pump functioning? Are you taking your meds? Are you eating properly? We won't climb Spoon Mountain with you if you're not at least in a modicum of shape."

"I eat great," I lied, surreptitiously chewing on a Kit Kat whose glucose overload was probably maiming my pancreas. "Each night I consult a Dean Ornish heart-friendly cookbook to rustle up another magical repast that eliminates bad cholesterol, lowers my blood pressure, scrubs all the plaque from my arteries, and makes my turds wheat-colored and buoyant in the bowl."

"Don't be a smart aleck, Dad. I recruited Ben and Jamie to cook you a special buffalo-meat-and-blueberries stew that I sent them the recipe for. You need protein and plenty of antioxidants."

"Buffalo meat and *blueberries*?"

Though Jamie is Ben's girlfriend she is not my favorite person. However, Ben loves her and if Ben loves her my lips are sealed forever. I think Jamie's a rigid bitch. Jamie doesn't have a sense of humor. She's *serious* all the time. She makes *plans*, everything is *orderly*, she speaks without using irony or sarcasm or slang. She never comprehends our jokes. She's like a Stepford wife. She can be a real fussbudget. She works for a title company. Even Sally says Jamie walks around with a poker up her ass, but Sally has to work with her. Apparently Jamie is competent. She has discipline. I will admit she's a good looker, tall and slim and very chic. She dresses *perfectly*. She's too chic, in fact. She reminds me of Brooke Shields. Beside her Ben could be one of the Three Stooges. I think Jamie is vapid and I hope Ben doesn't marry her. If he does marry her I'll bless them both and never say another word. I just hope I live long enough to catch the bouquet.

Ben is loyal. And also disciplined. As far as I know Jamie is the only girlfriend he has ever had. He's solid. When Ben decides to do something he does it to perfection. He thinks a lot before making a decision. And once he made the decision about Jamie he would have stuck up for her even if she was the CEO of Enron or Osama bin Laden's right-hand mujahedin.

"Of course he's loyal," Miranda told me once during her early teenage years. "Ben grew up in the family of a dysfunctional womanizer. Why would he want to be like you?"

"Dysfunctional" is a word Miranda threw around a lot when she hit puberty. That and the phrase: "You are so. Not. With it. Dad."

Funny thing is, for all her surface bluster, fast talk, and bawdy chatter, Miranda is probably more loyal than Ben. And even more disciplined than either Ben or Jamie.

Miranda will have a glass of wine at dinner, but only one glass, that's enough. She hasn't smoked a doobie since entering nursing school. Ben doesn't drink or smoke at all. He doesn't swear, either. He likes to stay in shape. He still rides his mountain bike on weekends. He even works out at the gym. I've asked him a few times if he and Jamie plan to have children. Ben's answer? "We're not ready for kids yet, Pop, we're not even married. We still have things to do. We need to grow up and learn to love each other better before we make those huge decisions."

Coming from anyone else, I might gag. Coming from my son, however, those words make perfect sense. Ben is not a prig and you can't argue with his decency. That would be like telling Paul Newman or Derek Jeter they are full of shit.

Five

"And tomorrow," Miranda said, "you should receive from me Priority Express a carton of vitamins that you have to take daily or I'm not climbing Spoon Mountain with you. Folic acid and magnesium, a box of those Emergen-C packets, B-12 and Ginkgo biloba. Are you eating a banana every day? You need the potassium."

"I eat two bananas every morning," I said, opening another Kit Kat and demolishing half of it with one chomp. "I also eat apples, pineapples, and passion fruits."

Miranda ignored my hyperbole, she always does. "If you don't eat properly, including those vitamins, Dad, nobody will climb that mountain with you. Ben and I are on the fence about this one so don't blow it. Not on our watch will you commit suicide on your sixty-fifth birthday if we can help it. Sixty-five is not thirty-five, hotshot."

"'Suicide'? We're simply taking a hike," I protested. No matter how I feel I *always* feign cavalier, that's the law of my jungle. "Relax. I climbed Spoon Mountain a hundred times when I was younger. You and Ben did too. It's a friendly little mountain, a molehill. It was *our* mountain, remember? And don't forget, we promised each other. Going back

15

up will be an important statement that needs to be made before this drought shuts everything down."

"A *statement*? Like what? Like when you exited open-heart surgery eleven years ago—remember that? If not let me refresh your memory. You were frozen blue and inflated like a balloon. Your features were unrecognizable. You had a breathing tube down your throat, a catheter up your penis, and IV needles stuck in both your arms which were strapped to the gurney at the wrists. I couldn't stop crying for hours. Ben went into the bathroom and upchucked. Even your ravishing fifth wife, the bipolar thespian, peed in her thong panties and had to be sedated with three Valiums and a Percodan. We don't need that kind of statement in this family ever again."

Good point.

It's not easy to argue with Miranda when you don't have a leg to stand on.

Six

In case you're getting the wrong impression, however, I had better explain something here. Over the years Miranda's basic way of loving me has been to vent all over me. I try not to take it personal. Actually, I do sometimes regret the way my daughter and I are trapped in playing the dozens. Who knows how that habit started or why we can't break it? I wish we could break it. The other night when I was lying in the dark with my heart going berserk I thought to myself: *Enough, already.* I want to sign a truce with Miranda before I expire. I don't think she acts that way with anyone else. Certainly not with her hubby Michael. Those two converse and even argue with each other like grown-ups. They are reasonable, loving, and patient with each other, never caustic. That said, I must admit Miranda and Lizzy get into it on occasion, which is no doubt my genes at work. Nonetheless, I'm struggling to quit blaming myself for everything. I need to make peace with my demons before it's too late. Doesn't everybody?

Therefore, let me say in my defense: I may have my faults but I am a *serious* human being. I care. I am an ecologist, a radical political person. And I've only been married and divorced three times, not five, thank you Miranda.

Let's not exaggerate my conjugal perfidies. And recognize that despite them I have had a long and quasi-distinguished professional career. I write literary fiction and thoughtful nonfiction essays. I have published sixteen books, that's not nothing. I also spent seventeen years working on over a dozen Hollywood screenplays for mostly respected directors attached to major studios. At age sixty-five I will begin collecting a pension from the Writers Guild of America (thank God!). That means I put in my time. I deserve it. I packed my lunch in a little black box and went to the steel mill five days a week for all those years.

You think I'm superficial because I only earned one credit and it was on a picture directed by Russ Meyer and starring Tura Satana? Well how about this: Three of my own early novels were turned into movies featuring some terrific actors who still amass their fair share of kudos. Besides Christopher Walken, other actors in the film version of *The Lucky Underdogs* are Freddy Fender and Melanie Griffith. *The Lucky Underdogs* was my third published novel and it has remained in print going on thirty years. Critics usually refer to it as "a regional classic." The *Denver Post* once decreed: "With luck, Jonathan Kepler may become the García Márquez of southwestern literature."

You see, I've had my fifteen minutes of fame. All the same, I never developed a swelled head or got rich. Though for story conferences movie studios have put me up at the Chateau Marmont, Manhattan's Helmsley Palace, and the Miami Beach Fontainebleau, I always hightailed it back to the Southwest and wrote all my scripts at home. That was specified in the contracts. Sure, Hollywood paid the bills;

no, it never snagged my soul. You can't impress me with the glitterati or material gain. I avoided the fast lane because I had other fish to fry far from the madding crowd.

To wit: I am also an outdoors man, an amateur naturalist, an exercise freak. I live in a spectacular physical setting you could call paradise if you ignored its bleak human socioeconomics, which I never have. When I used to pitch films in L.A. I tried to sum up the story in one paragraph aimed at three Cardin suits blowing Cohiba smoke in my face. Today if I had to plug my town as a movie to a trio of impatient producers looking for its hook I would probably say: "This burg is all about Climax Tourism versus Abject Poverty in a multiracial gangbang located in a Shangri-La rapidly being overdeveloped and undernourished by legions of greedy former hippie in-migrants with PhDs who've lost their moral compasses and a bunch of indigenous folk eager to obliterate their historical mandate for moola." Other than that I'll abstain from discussing my village, per se, in this book, because I've beaten that dog to death elsewhere, I'm sorry. Read *The Lucky Underdogs* if you want a humorous (and tragic) guided tour through the main streets, back alleys, and corrupt politics running our economy and our environment into the ground; that's not where I'm headed this time out of the gate. Even Trotsky donned his striped woolen bathing costume and went to the beach on Saturday after training the Red Army all week. What you are about to read is a personal, *intimate* story by the New Me, not a comical tract about how to organize the proletariat to cast off its chains and build a working-class utopia. Been there, done that, old tapes.

Suffice it to say, my little haven is a picturesque rural ghetto bordered on the west by empty sagebrush mesa. The Río Grande Gorge cuts through the middle of this breathtaking high desert plain. I have fly-fished that gorge since we moved out west from New York in 1969 and I am no slouch with an Irresistible. I would much rather be angling at home than networking the West Coast goniffs. East of town tall mountains rise above 13,000 feet and I've spent decades traipsing among them. Maybe not lately, it's true. I fell off the wagon during the farce of my last marital travesty (with Wife #3, the "bipolar thespian"), which was highlighted by a nearly fatal endocarditis infection inside my heart, followed by congestive heart failure, open-heart surgery to repair my blown-out mitral valve, and four subsequent cardioversions, then a lifetime supply of Digitalis. It was a harrowing experience and I beat the rap anyway. At least so far so good. Knock on wood.

That said, I used to be the Jeremiah Johnson (*and* the John Muir) of the Sangre de Cristos, ask anyone. The Sangre de Cristo Mountains east of town. I often climbed Gavilán Peak backward, feeding peanuts to the marmots en route. For a spell I ate Spoon Mountain for breakfast. My kids came along for the ride during their summer vacations with me after their mother (Wife #1) divorced me. That was the whole point of moving out west from New York in the first place. I wanted my children to experience the real world of spruce forests, wild mammals, and migratory birds. We carried a spotting scope for tracking the bighorn sheep along their precarious clifftop routes. We squawked at ravens circling above us and admired elk gathered in alpine meadows during September snow flurries. Believe me, Hollywood can't hold a candle to this terrain, not even during these days of drought when you're more apt to choke on forest fire smoke in September than to flee from early autumn snowstorms. Anymore it might not begin snowing until *after* Christmas.

Ben and Miranda camped with me at Gallegos Lake, a beautiful turquoise puddle at 11,000 feet. It's pristine. We had fun fishing and climbing the peaks around us, especially Spoon Mountain, our favorite. We were a mini von Trapp family gamboling across the Alps. My heart was indomitable before it sprang a leak. Miranda once said, "Daddy, you're so strong you'll never die unless you canoodle yourself into a date with the morgue at an early age." Where did *that* lingo come from? She was only eleven or twelve but must have been sneaking peeks at my Damon Runyon stories. Ben rolled up like a hedgehog whenever Miranda used weird language. He is not adept at colorful metaphors. Ben is an enormous gentle giant who flinches if you say, "What are you looking at, buddy?" He would not hurt a flea. You can bounce rocks off his head all day with no fear he'll retaliate. You can call him names, that's water off his back. You can't hassle his sister or his girlfriend, though. He will ask you politely to stop. If you don't stop, he will kill you. So far that has never happened because when Ben asks you to stop, you stop.

Seven

I really hate telephones but I can't avoid answering them, especially not these days. Maybe it will be my New York agent, perhaps a Hollywood producer, possibly some college offering me fifteen hundred bucks for a speech about how my novel *The Lucky Underdogs* was turned into a film, and I'm not proud anymore, I'll take it. Sadly, my financial assets are not what they used to be. When I had it I flaunted it, I gave it away, money embarrasses me, it makes me feel guilty. Why? Because too many people don't have it. I lost the rest of my winnings to three wives in three divorces. Easy come, easy go. How did I earn it? Pickin' cotton.

"Can I come over, baby? I'm going off my rocker. I won't stay long, Scout's honor."

Politely I said, "Maybe another time, Sally. I'm trying to kick back and mellow out for a change. It's part of 'getting in shape' for Spoon Mountain. Right now I'm sitting outside paying attention to the flowers. You wouldn't understand or be interested. I used to be so close to nature and then I sluffed off in the last few years. I got lazy. Now I'm going back before it's too late. I promised my children. We all have to renew our ecological contracts or it's curtains."

Be advised: Sally is verbose, I am verbose, and so is my daughter, Miranda. All three of us graduated from the University of Loquacity. We don't speak in clipped sentences when we open our mouths, we speak in speeches. We are emphatic. We want to make sure everyone gets the point. Hence, you should understand this is not going to be a book with dialogue by Ernest Hemingway. In real life people don't talk like that anyway. Forewarned is forearmed.

So: Sally has buttons, and if you push them, be prepared.

"What do you mean I 'wouldn't understand'? Speak for yourself, nene. I have a brain too, in case you hadn't noticed. We'll mellow out together. I'll bring champagne. A few minutes with me won't kill you, I just need a hug. You won't believe what has happened the last few days. I had the whole Mandelman deal locked up, signed, sealed, you name it. I mean creative financing like you never saw before in your life. Half of it from the mortgage company, half from the bank, and sixty thousand held by the seller with a twenty K balloon payment every two years, and the transaction fell apart at closing because the buyers decided to get divorced. Excuse me? Am I hearing correctly? Yes, they started bickering right in front of all of us at the title company, she called him a geek, he called her a flaming bitch, and they both walked out. It cost me a fifteen grand commission and that's not the half of it. Zachary was busted for shoplifting a Tupac CD at Walmart two days ago and Alex announced last night at dinner that he intends to quit high school his senior year. When I asked 'Why?' he said 'Cause I'm bored.' You know what his dad said? 'Go for it, Alex.' Where does that man get his priorities? We also have another budding crisis situation at home. Jason, who has possessed his driver's license for all of two hair-raising weeks, had a fender bender in the Furr's lot on Saturday with Magistrate Judge Rosalie Nesbitt's grandmother. And I had one more deal that bit the dust late yesterday when the buyer, this overweight person from Lubbock, discovered there's asbestos poisoning the ceiling. Asbestos? I didn't know that. He hired Max González to do a separate private inspection, and Max is always undercutting my people because I wouldn't do his woody in a backseat five years ago during the Lawrence Festival. I am so sick of trying to unload overpriced houses onto clueless rich people. You think your job is difficult, amor, you ought to try selling property in this market to the crowd that wants it and can afford to pay the outrageously inflated prices."

Then you wait a moment to see if that's all. If it is, you reply glumly: "Okay, I guess."

"Okay, what?"

"Okay, I guess you can come over here, Sally. I mean, I couldn't stop you if I wanted to, could I?"

"Should I bring my ice ax and my pitons?" she giggled.

Eight

Of course, Sally doesn't own an ice ax or pitons. She is not antiexercise, however. Sally stays in shape. Her body is lovely. Tantalizing. She eats carefully. She doesn't smoke cigarettes yet likes to chill with a leño and a glass of wine after work. She goes to Curves three evenings a week and works out with an Abdominizer at home. She owns several Jane Fonda and Cory Everson workout tapes. I am a big fan of Cory Everson. Sally will look at birds through binoculars on walks with me as long as we don't go uphill. She has an aversion to inclines.

Sally also has more energy for healthy sex than many women I've known. If I give her a come-hither sign she's all over me like a box of kittens. I can barely manage to keep her at bay without another half tab of Viagra. Sally figures that good sex is God's way of apologizing for tornadoes, hurricanes, and the Holocaust. I'm sorry to say that she actually *believes* in God. No, she doesn't believe in heaven or hell or the Holy Trinity, but she was baptized Catholic and wears a little gold crucifix on a delicate chain around her neck. To be sure, Sally never goes to church, she can't stand the endless incantations of the octogenarian Rosary Girls. Yet I'm not allowed to trash the Pope, not even over birth control despite the fact that she bought condoms for each of her boys the minute their voices changed. Nevertheless, God pops out of her mouth on a regular basis. "God will get you for that." Or: "Shut up, God hates a whiner." Or: "If God had meant for Texans to ski He would have given them mountains."

Though Sally abhors Texans she keeps her trap closed about them because they buy most of the houses she earns a commission on. She believes firmly that "I'll rot in hell for selling houses, pero a mi no me importa. I have other stuff to worry about." She makes way more money than I do. She spends it too. The lady is extravagant up to a point. After that it's all about Jason, Alex, and Zachary. She is a river to her offspring.

Sally likes it when I tie her up with velvet ropes or gag her with a silver scarf. She enjoys being lewd, vulgar, and profane as long as we don't take it too seriously. If you can't laugh, don't fuck. She thinks I'm a "randy old goat." Naturally I agree, although at my age it's not easy to keep abreast. At least I don't wear a toupée. Whenever we indulge ourselves I wind up in atrial fibrillation and have to lie on my back on the bed with my feet high on the wall while executing the Valsalva maneuver. That's where you push down straining as if constipated which hopefully will stop your heart so it can recommence in sinus rhythm. Some of my more finicky inamoratas have disliked these melodramatic postcoital affects, but Sally generally takes them in stride.

"If you die I'll call Ben," she says.

"Don't call Ben, call Miranda."

"How come? Ben lives only three minutes away."

"You don't understand, Sally. Call Miranda. Ben is not big on female hysteria."

We do have fun together. Sally's sense of humor is whimsical. Yes, she laughs at Abbott and Costello movies; no, she cannot abide old Monty Python episodes on late-night television. She adored those Stupid Pet Tricks on David Letterman, but hated *Third Rock from the Sun*. She loves telenovelas on SIN and despises soap operas in English. Sally is a wonderful cook. I don't know how she does it. Though she could throw TV dinners at her boys after a day at work, she makes enchiladas instead, or delicious tacos, or jumbo shrimps sautéed in garlic and basil. It barely takes her nanoseconds on Friday evenings to feed her three JDs, shoo them out the door to party on with their criminal homies, and look like a million dollars five minutes later when I show up for *my* dinner and a glass of wine.

Sidebar: Although Sally and I have been a quasi-item for over a year I don't mingle with Alex, Zachary, and Jason. I arrive at their digs when Sally informs me the coast is clear; the lads rarely return until I am already history. That is for Sally's protection as well as my own. We abstain from the nasties at her house because little pitchers have big ears, and, Sally says, "There's no point in giving Don the Man more ammo than he already possesses. If you ever ask me to marry you in a church that's a different story. Then I won't be a hooker in his eyes, corrupting our precious offspring, I'll be an honest woman. Believe it or not, Don could deal with that. He's a born-again who attends mass with a rosary in each fist and a crucifix between his teeth."

Sally was married once before her Don the Man debacle. Also to an Anglo who turned out to be a loser. "I don't know why I choose bigoted gabachos," she says. "It's a serious flaw in my makeup. Who knows why I chose real estate, either. My father was a respectable dentist in El Paso, my mother worked in a bank. My brother is a veterinarian. As a kid I dreamed of being the next Cristina Saralegui with my own talk show in English and Spanish, interviewing Marisol and Julio Iglesias. Mom wanted me to become a famous golfer like Nancy López."

Sally is a really good golfer. I do not like golf. Still, I enjoy watching her play. I carry her bag on practice rounds or even during the club tournament. We walk for the exercise instead of using a cart. I never say a word, those are the rules, and Sally does not talk either. For once she is mute. On the golf course nothing disturbs her concentration. Sally studies golf. She watches it on the telly over the yowls of Alex, Zachary, and Jason, who would rather be tuned in to *Dog, The Bounty Hunter*. Occasionally after work Sally will go directly from the office to the club driving range to hit a few buckets of balls. I'll meet her there and have a drink at the bar afterward. What is it called, the Nineteenth Hole? No, I would not join the club if you forced me at gunpoint. Nevertheless, I like the driving range, a patch of luxuriant green grass surrounded by sagebrush mesa with snowcapped mountains in the background. Or they used to be snowcapped, you know, before the planet tanked. There are no trees or houses anywhere near the club. It's an incredible setting if you forget about all the water dumped on the desert to keep it verdant while our town enforces

Stage 2 water restrictions. My girl won't hear of that, however. The subject is off-limits, taboo, verboten.

Sally says, "When I'm out here in the middle of nowhere hitting a Titleist ball a hundred and fifty yards, I feel like a king."

"You mean a queen."

Sally reached over and gave me that little index-finger tickle under my chin, her eyes impertinent. "Whatever you say, sweetie pie," she said. "After all, you're my man, aren't you? Theoretically speaking, at least. Or after a fashion, I suppose?"

Nine

Obediently, I opened the bottle of Freixenet Sally brought and poured two glasses, asking myself: How come I always get in too deep with provocative women who drive me batty? What's wrong with me? I'm not an inherently bad person nor a completely indiscriminate lover, am I? Sally may be flashy and opinionated, but she is also a class act and, frankly, a trophy girlfriend any guy worth his salt would want on his arm in a pinch. The fact that she tolerates me is a great blessing of my recent existence. So why am I so afraid of her? Naturally, it goes without saying that I'm terrified of commitment. At my age, with my track record, why shouldn't I be? I have *been* married. On the other hand, at my age and with my track record you'd think a woman like Sally would be heaven sent and I'd be a fool not to latch onto her. I'm an old codger and she still exudes a girlish gleam. Yet what if I married her and then *she* took a powder? It's happened before. I can't let myself be engulfed by an emotional trap. I hate to be confined. What if I lose Sally, though, how could I ever begin anew with another woman? Or why would I even want to . . . unless I'd die without the erotic stimulation? But do you *have* to sign on the line?

To be honest, I am not enraptured by the thought of getting hitched to Sally in a church or anywhere else, for that matter. There's no denying I've been married three times, yet I don't even *believe* in marriage. My second and third weddings were near-fatal accidents caused by animal excess and illegal drugs leading to irrational behavior I lived to regret. What did Engels say about marriage in a patriarchal capitalist society? He said, "Don't do it, you'll live to regret it." Amen to that.

So I'm torn. There is a new sense of foreboding in my life that makes me anxious. Hungry wolves are gathering on the edge of my perimeter. Have I segued into my own end game?

I lugged another white plastic chair outside for Sally, planting it beside my own chair in front of the small flower garden underneath my kitchen window. "Garden" is a euphemism. I dug in a batch of bulbs and stuff willy-nilly fourteen years ago and each spring and summer ever since it's been sauve qui peut among the survivors. I pump gray water from the tub through a hose to this green patch: The rest of my lot has become a dust bowl. I have two cats, Cookie (the gray one) and her brother Carlos (the black one). They were asleep in the garden, curled up together among some poppies. They are old cats, that's about all they do, they sleep.

La novia nibbled my earlobe then partitioned a chocolate éclair from the bakery at Bob's Diner in town and handed me my half as she settled languorously beside me gazing at the bright red poppies, the happy daisies, the irises about to bloom. Despite my rotten heart I'm addicted to the pastries from Bob's Diner, an eatery that looms large in my legend, though not for the reasons you might think. I'll explain as we go along. The day was hot and smoggy, you could smell the statewide forest fires burning out of control. That made me wonder: When would the Feds close down the local wilderness because of fire danger caused by the drought? The Arctic is melting, the Sahara expanding, and the northern part of my state is beginning to look like southern Arizona. Already, bears are descending from the mountains because there aren't any berries up higher. People shoot the bears when they tip over their garbage cans or plastic dumpsters. Humanity's nature hatred is suicidal. I love bears and can't stand their situation. Bears are the canaries in *my* coal mine.

Sally had on a tight blue long-sleeved jersey to die for and beige short shorts and sandals: Some cookie. I have to admit Sally is beautiful. She must have been a knockout at eighteen, she is a knockout at almost fifty, and I know she will be a knockout at seventy-five. She has pretty ears, small, with almost no lobes, but likes large jangly earrings. She is shapely and only five-two. She has greenish eyes. Her upper lip protrudes very slightly over her lower lip in the suggestion of a pout. An alluring pout. Her hair is a light brunette with almost an auburn tint because her grandfather came from Galicia in northern Spain where people are descended from Celts. She has a lovely neck and wider shoulders than you might expect and exquisite collarbones. Put bluntly, Sally is DDG. Ask my granddaughter Lizzy what that means, she'll tell you in a New York minute.

We clinked our glasses. "Here's lookin' at you, kid." Sally

torched a doobie and took a puff but I declined because I was "in training," paying rapt attention to three elm beetles negotiating the hairs of poppy sepals and to a white-lined sphinx moth buzzing at the phlox while nearby a small black weevil sawed through a wild sunflower twig with its vicious little proboscis.

Zen and the art of insect watching. If you haven't tried it, don't knock it. I may have strayed from the straight and narrow over the last two decades but my heart still belongs to nature. That is in our genes even if we don't acknowledge it. It's *inherent*. Though I won't hector the point here, please keep it in mind during the rest of this narrative because it forms the invisible underside of my iceberg throughout. If we don't salvage the environment, social justice is beside the point. End of lecture.

My girlfriend grew restless. Sally appreciates nature in the abstract, but she is not an enviro proctologist. She said, "This is boring," and squibbed the cell phone from her pocket and stared at it hoping to telepathically make it tootle. I smiled, saying, "Please put that thing away, sweetie, okay?" Sally said, "No, sweetie, this is my livelihood, it saves me." I quit smiling and said, "I can't stand that cell phone, okay?" She said, "No, not 'okay' Mr. Self-righteous Lefty Luddite unless you intend to marry me and adopt my three teenage progeny and commit to paying their health insurance, upcoming college tuitions, and car payments also."

Touché. We've had this argument before. I stifled, shifting my gaze to some ants milking aphids on the stem of a rosebush.

Sally softened up, which she often does immediately

after nailing me with a cutting riposte. Be careful, however. Sally regularly communicates on three levels at once. Face value is not her verbal copilot.

"You hate me, don't you?" she said. "I know you despise my job and its exploitational nature. Well, I don't blame you. I hate it, too. I have to lie to my clients, selling crap as if it was crème brûlée. That's no fun. Some nights I lie awake wondering how else I could earn a living and gain a bit of stature in your eyes. You're only in it for the sex with me, I bet."

"Of course I really love the sex," I admitted. "But I also like—"

Her cell phone bleeped obnoxiously:

"Listen, Gilbert, listen up carefully," Sally said. "I'm only going to say this once because it's after office hours and I'm enjoying myself on an adventure in wild nature. Linda told me there are two covenants on the land, only two. The buyers cannot build until they pay the second balloon and own the property outright. And they cannot put a commercial business on it that would affect the residential neighborhood. Also, the present title company won't insure the right-of-way. Black Dog Surveying is researching that problem. The Johnsons won't sign an easement? I think that's bogus posturing. The road has to be public domain. Now if you'll excuse me I have to commune with the larger cosmos. Adiós, muchito."

I said, "I'll bet there isn't a cell phone on top of Spoon Mountain, what do you think?"

Sally frowned at me and I prepared to duck. But she fooled me. You can never grow complacent with her.

"I honestly don't care what isn't on top of that peak, querido. I hate to say it, but when you come off that mountain, if you survive, I would honestly just like you to love me and then take me away from all of this. Is that so hard to understand? I'm tired." She reached over and squiggled her fingers against the nape of my neck. "Come down from your Ivory Tower and make me an offer I can't refuse. Quit being such a scaredy-cat."

A fat raven who alighted on a nearby Siberian elm branch gabbled and quorked a few times and I croaked and clucked right back at it, doing okay on the deep throat rattles and not so good on the aspirate H. I've been talking to ravens for years though I don't know if they understand me or even if *I* know what I'm saying. Makes no difference. The palaver forges a bond, however blurry. Maybe this bird had been attracted to my house because of pheromones drifting off the éclair from Bob's Diner, an allusion you will comprehend presently. Sally thinks I'm daft when I speak to ravens so she rolled her eyes to the sky—*oh spare me, homes!*—and bussed me lasciviously right on the mouth.

At that precise moment Fate interceded and changed my life completely. Out the corner of my eye I noticed Don the Man's tulip-red extended-cab Ford pickup slowing for the speed hump on Valverde Street as Don did a double take . . . and then he peeled away in a real hissy fit.

Given my luck I could almost guarantee what would happen next. I just didn't know when.

Ten

No, I have never personally met Don the Man, although I've seen him driving around town in his big fat pickup truck with booster shocks elevating its hind end. He wears black T-shirts, has a strand of blue barbwire tattooed around each bicep, and his greasy blond hair is twisted into dorky Rasta dreads he thinks are cool. He is three years younger than Sally and, according to her, a truly fun-loving sexy guy . . . with serious anger-management issues that never boiled over until after Zachary was born. Don thought breast-feeding Zachary would ruin Sally's figure and he was jealous of Zack for taking away his wife's attention. "Typical macho crap," Sally said. That's how it started. She and her volatile hubby had an up-down relationship until Sally finally obtained a restraining order, filed for divorce, and began studying for her real estate license. Sally is a survivor. She's always the last person voted off the island. The first time she told Don the Man to go stuff his child support because she had closed a big-dollar deal he went over the edge. She should not have done that. Sally is smart, she's very tough, and she can also be reckless. One of her major personality quirks is that she is attracted to heels, con men, guys who cheat on her. Not that she is a professional victim. "I'm simply an optimist," she admits. "I always assume, well, *this* Romeo is going to sweep me off my feet, buy me a Frigidaire, and be nice to my kids."

As for yours truly? Despite my progressive politics I attended the same emotional school as Sally. I've dealt with enough flamboyant un-PC behavior in my day to last a lifetime. So what? I say we are all walking contradictions. Though married, Karl Marx impregnated his housekeeper on the side. I'll wager Mahatma Gandhi secretly diddled chorus girls. Same as Sally, I'm a degenerate. I am drawn to volcanic voluptuous women. Kepler's Second Law of Motion according to Miranda applies. Growing up I was fascinated by the tempestuous Italian movie actresses Anna Magnani, Sophia Loren, and Silvana Mangano. *Boy on a Dolphin. The Rose Tattoo.* Sexy comediennes, drama queens, and erotic neurotics turn me on. Anger—threats, sobs, shrieks, and physical mayhem—is an aphrodisiac. On a book tour once (in Chicago) I was briefly jailed when an inebriated groupie threw a ceramic lamp out of our downtown hotel window at 4:00 a.m. just for kicks. I have never been infatuated with a stable person. When I was younger that was fun; nowadays I seem to be running out of oomph. I could use a little bourgeois peace and quiet in a relationship . . . if it didn't cost too much. I am not a born accommodator although chances are I would not have kicked Amy Winehouse out of bed. See what I mean?

Miranda tells me, "You're a child, Papa-san. I mean it. You don't know the first thing about love or intimacy. Ben and I are light-years ahead of you. You're going to die in the gutter a bum and nobody will give a damn. Except me. I love you. You're my favorite oxymoron."

Yes, Miranda can deliver a harsh opinion; no, she is not a neutral person. We already know that. Truth is, however, Miranda could fill the shoes of Mother Teresa and she does not believe in God either. When she was eleven she caught Ben reading the Bible and ordered him to throw it away. He did not want to chuck it. Ben was a mysterious child. Miranda said if he did not bag the Bible he would suffer brain damage and wind up flaying himself with birch whips. Ben is stubborn. He jutted his lower jaw at her.

So Miranda said, "You're kidding me. You believe that God talks out of a burning bush? You believe Jesus could feed ten thousand people with one loaf of bread? You believe human beings get turned into pillars of salt when God snaps Her fingers? You believe God dried up the Red Sea so Moses could walk across it? You think God drowned everybody on earth by making it rain for a month?"

I don't know where Miranda received all her information because I never took the kids to church. Neither did their mother. We are atheists. We did not discuss religion in our household. Until Sally, I had never even dated a Christian, God forbid, although aside from being a depressed bad actress my third wife was a lapsed Catholic who dabbled in a local coven for a spell (no pun intended). The only occasions when I enter a church are to deliver eulogies at friends' funerals. I'm good at that. "Keep it short, bub," the Catholic priest, Father Rumaldo, tells me. You can smell the schnapps on his breath. His covert mistress is our magistrate judge, Rosalie Nesbitt, whose husband,

Randall Nesbitt, the oblivious cuckold, is a sheriff's deputy. And don't forget Rosalie's grandmother who got fender-bended in the Furr's parking lot by Sally's third out of the womb, Jason, a few days ago. Jason is short, bald, and thinks he's Eminem. His brother Zachary is tall, bald, and thinks he's Kid Rock without hair. He is the kleptomaniac. Their brother Alex is tall, with hair down to his waist, and he thinks he's Marilyn Manson. He wears mascara and Salmon Pink lipstick. My girlfriend tells me Rosalie Nesbitt's granny is a sinister herbalist who used to treat Don the Man for his lumbago with a compress made from eye of endangered newt and spadefoot toad tongues. It's a small southwestern mountain town, get used to it.

By the time Miranda finished admonishing Ben for reading the scriptures he was crying. I think he picked up a Bible in the first place because he'd had enough of life inside my secular temple of Eros and wanted more solid dreck to hold onto.

"Trust me," Miranda told him. "I understand your problem, but God is not the answer." Then she gave him a big hug. Miranda was the only person who could hug Ben and get away with it. After a certain age (maybe six) if anyone else tried to envelop him in their arms Ben squirmed, horribly embarrassed and confused. I don't know where that comes from. I myself have always embraced people, especially women, with great fervor.

Eleven

Speaking of Ben, the next thing I knew he and his girl-friend Jamie appeared on my kitchen stoop carrying a cardboard box that held ten plastic yogurt containers of buffalo meat stew that had masking tape labels on the lids indicating the date I should consume their contents right up until my birthday. Ben's dog Cujo leaped from the truck bed and chased my cats Cookie and Carlos up a tree, then he flounced into the kitchen beside his master and devoured all their cat food. I almost pasted the hound yet restrained myself. It's the New Me. Cujo is missing most of his left ear because a starving bear swatted it off last summer while raiding the lone apple tree in Ben's tiny yard. Later, three city cops (aided by sheriff's deputy Randall Nesbitt) cornered the bear behind Wendy's and blew it to kingdom come. Their picture, with feet planted atop the dead bear, was on the front page of our weekly newspaper. Cujo is part German shepherd, part German SS, but Ben rescued him from the animal shelter and smothers him with love, who knows why? Ben nurtures a soft spot for emotional cripples. It runs in the family. His mother's second husband was an alcoholic with CFS. Her third hubby had PTSD after Vietnam. I had been 4-F and proud of it.

I marched on the Pentagon in 1967. If I'd had a flower I would have stuck it in a gun barrel PDQ.

My son is not the sort of person who wastes much time lollygagging and making small talk. He led Cujo by the collar out to his truck and locked him in the cab while Jamie gave me directions.

"All you have to do is thaw a carton and dump the stew into a pot and ignite a burner. One jar equals one meal. Remove it from the freezer when you wake up. Are you drinking plenty of soy milk?"

Ben returned to the kitchen followed shortly by Cookie and Carlos who shot through the cat door and disappeared into the bedroom where they always seek refuge in my closet after being traumatized.

"What is this goulash made of?" I asked, inspecting a container. Ben had on his usual construction duds and Jamie looked extra cute in bleached 501 jeans, a gray sweatshirt, and a spiffy blue beret. Even though I can't stand her personality, physically she turns me on.

"It has lentils, carrots, tofu, celery, onions, garlic, basil, sea salt, free-range buffalo meat from South Dakota that I found at the co-op, and blueberries from Maine. The blueberries are rich in antioxidants. All the ingredients are organic."

I said, "Wow. I imagine this stuff is delicious."

Ben said, "Don't be sarcastic, Pop. You should eat it even if you hate it. Did you get the vitamins Miranda sent?"

I swung open a cabinet door above the sink and gestured at the shiny new bottles in a pretty row: "Voilà."

Ben unsheathed his Leatherman, flicked forth the

knife blade, reached up, and one by one he slowly cut off the plastic safety wrappers around the bottle caps so they could actually be opened.

"You shouldn't let things sit here growing mold," he said. "If Miranda learns you're doing that we probably won't climb Spoon Mountain with you. Personally, I think we should not hike right now but at least you could make a small effort. Miranda will bring an oxygen bottle and one of those portable battery-operated defibrillator kits on our trek. However, it would be excellent if we don't have to use them."

The thing about Ben is he knows medicine. He understands life-threatening situations. He is hypersensitive to illness in other people and exudes special compassion for them. Ben is diabetic. Type 1 juvenile onset diabetes. The summer he turned eleven he and Miranda were with me, per the divorce agreement, and we were having a blast until Ben commenced pissing rivers and sucking up water like a fire truck at a six-alarm blaze. Miranda, who was only nine, caught on immediately.

"There's something wrong with Ben," she said.

"He looks okay," I said. "How do you feel, Ben?"

Ben shrugged and nodded. Miranda said, "Talk out loud."

"I'm okay, I feel great," her brother said.

"He's not great," Miranda insisted. "He never drinks water like this. He's turning into a fish."

"No I'm not. I'm okay," Ben said.

Miranda grew really concerned. "Something is *wrong*," she said. "You better call Mom or I'm calling the police."

"I can't call your mother every time you get a flea in your ear," I said. "I'm supposed to be taking care of you guys. She doesn't want to hear about our squabbles. This is her vacation time away from you little thugs. I'm in charge here and Ben says he's okay and I believe him."

Miranda's eyes narrowed. They are green like Sally's but more intense, almost emerald. I'm talking about a nine-year-old little girl here. When Miranda wanted to she could evolve instantly into a Child of the Corn or a Demon Seed. Her motto right from birth was, "Nobody messes with me."

Nevertheless, I could tell she was confused. Ben was not backing her up. Ben seemed to be an all-American healthy boy. He looked super. He was not in pain. So Miranda retreated. She walked outside in a huff casting suspicious backward glances at her brother and defiant angry glances at me.

Fifteen minutes later their mother called from the Capital City to ask me, "What is the matter with Ben? How come you aren't taking him to a doctor?"

Obviously, Miranda had gone next door to a phone at the neighbor's house and ratted me out.

"It's Saturday," I said. "I'll make an appointment on Monday."

"Take him to the emergency room," she ordered. "Now."

One reason for our breakup was that tone of voice. Never have I responded well to authority. True, many people have addressed me in that derogatory way and usually I deserved it. Ben and Miranda's mother is a no-nonsense person. We got married because I was blinded by her brains, her beauty, and her left-wing intransigence, and she was blinded by my good looks, my puerile sense of humor, and my antiwar ardor. Back then she was SDS and I was *almost* CPUSA. We made an attractive couple, we both spoke French, and our tennis matches against each other were epic. Too, my early success as a writer in New York didn't hurt.

Still, that woman has no tolerance for being stepped on. Six minutes after learning about my first affair (it happened at the Chateau Marmont, I'm afraid, while I was polishing a picture for Costa-Gavras), she filed for a separation. She had kicked me out of our Upper Ranchitos house and thrown my belongings into the irrigation ditch even before I finished explaining that it would never happen again. I wound up with the property, though, because my wife hated this town and wanted to move to the Capital City for more action. Today she is a prominent divorce lawyer. If it had not been for Hollywood I could never have paid her her share of the Upper Ranchitos house. Then I lost the place anyway, the second time around, to the wife Miranda always refers to as "Dolly Parton," which is not a compliment.

I chastised Miranda all the way to the emergency room. Then I had to eat an enormous portion of crow when they informed me Ben had type 1 diabetes. The doctors congratulated me for alertly catching it before Ben had entered DKA. That means diabetic ketoacidosis. It's when there is a major lapse of insulin moderating the glucose in your body.

I'm still trying to live down my behavior that day. To her everlasting credit, once Ben's illness was diagnosed and people were taking care of him, Miranda never pulled an "I-told-you-so" on me. Instead, she grew quiet and, on reflection, I believe she must have understood how bad I felt and made a conscious decision not to rub it in. Unusual behavior for a child. The past few days I have been thinking about that. I mean, as far as I know Miranda has never stopped loving me despite my many shortcomings. I am still her favorite oxymoron. Or at least I hope so. Maybe it will turn out that there is more forgiveness on earth than you can shake a stick at. My fingers are crossed.

Ben was perplexed when we began shooting him full of insulin four or five times daily and forbade him to eat Cocoa Puffs. All the same, he did not complain. Not that he is a martyr, no way. Ben is like a wild animal that simply curls up when it's hurt. You never really know how much he hurts because Ben is always quiet. He *never* makes a fuss.

Twelve

hile Ben was slicing off plastic wrappers Jamie had stacked the yogurt cartons in my freezer. Then she checked the main refrigerator compartment which displayed a cellophane-window carryout box with two strawberry cream puffs from Bob's Diner in it, four Tecates, and a half cantaloupe still covered by Saran Wrap with blotches of green penicillin decorating its orangey pink meat.

"Yuck."

She extricated the cantaloupe, dropping it in a wastebasket under the sink, then pointed her finger at the cream puffs: "These will kill you." Duh.

Ben and Jamie don't eat tref. They're not vegans, I'm happy to say, in fact Ben would snout down a horse if you barbecued it properly. But they never load up on sweets because of Ben's diabetes, and also because even if you didn't have diabetes the caramel cupcakes and chocolate frosted creme-filled donuts from the Bob's Diner bakeshop tend to knock you for a loop. They give me tachycardia attacks that I subdue with the Valsalva maneuver. I suspect many of Bob's grandiose pastries wind up half-eaten in the two commercial dumpsters without lids behind the restaurant where you can usually find a phalanx of greedy ravens dining on every jettisoned edible from soup to hay. More about these ravens soon.

Next, Jamie directed her scorn toward a nearby tub of kitty litter in my kitchen.

"Do you *ever* empty this cat box?" she asked.

"Sometimes I forget for a few days," I admitted, eager to expel them before they discovered some reason to ditch Spoon Mountain and commit me to the Living Center over behind Holy Cross Hospital. These days, surprise visitors to my raunchy digs are never exactly welcome, least of all family members, especially female family members who tend to disapprove of my somewhat—shall we say casual?—housekeeping. When you've been batching it as long as I have the physical plant tends to grow a bit gnarly. My kitchen looks like the aftermath of an F5 tornado. I am not proud of that, especially not when I'm trying to convince everybody I'm as capable as Sir Edmund Hillary. I don't want Miranda or Ben or even Jamie to start thinking that my outer appearances are a reflection of my inner competence or lack of same. What they don't know won't hurt me.

"'A few days?'" Jamie removed her beret and scratched her curly locks. "It looks to me as if your cats have been using that same litter for a year."

My first instinct was to tell Jamie to go take a flying douche at a rolling donut. That would have been an inappropriate response. Even though he and Jamie aren't married yet, it might have prompted Ben to pick me up, turn me upside down, and cram my head into the toilet. No, my son is not vindictive, however you don't want to goad him unnecessarily. Besides, I already felt like a man with one foot in the grave so why tickle the dragon's tail? My goal was to climb Spoon Mountain on my sixty-fifth birthday with Ben and Miranda, period. If I had to fawn in order to accomplish this I would fawn. You haven't seen a real toady's performance until you've caught my act on the hustings. Step aside, Uriah Heep, let a pro show you how to writhe unctuously.

I smiled at Jamie, grabbed a fork, and began spooning kitty turds into the wastebasket. I apologized for my absent-mindedness. "Won't happen again," I promised. Hearing my hustling and bustling, Cookie and Carlos meandered in from the other room and sat down on silent haunches five feet away from me, obviously happy to see their commode being scrubbed. What next, brand-new catnip mice from the pet department at Walmart? Oh goody.

"Thank you, thank you for all the wonderful food," I said, guiding Ben and his fiancée firmly toward the kitchen door. When I opened it you could smell the forest fire smoke lying across our valley. If they close the national forest I'll kill myself.

"It's not enough to thank us," Ben cast back over one shoulder as they headed for his truck. "Remember, you have to eat it, okay?"

Thirteen

I ate it, all right, for lunch the next day, an entire yogurt container of free-range buffalo meat stew teeming with antioxidants. The concoction tasted delicious, very spicy. Then everything went wrong behind my abdominal wall and I spent the next two hours scooting back and forth to the bathroom plagued by a virulent diarrhea. Naturally, my heart clicked into A-fib and I couldn't get it out with the Valsalva maneuver. Too bad. I had an engagement to perform at my pal Aaron Osborne's bookstore, I have fans, I never disappoint them even if only for a hundred bucks paid under the table, not at this late stage of my waning career. Gone are the days when checks for ten or fifteen thousand dollars arrived from Warner Brothers or Universal with regularity. Just think of me now as Sally Field wearing a ton of pancake makeup hawking bone density supplements on late-night TV. So, dying or not, my pal Aaron's establishment is where I went.

The smarmier side of our tony tourist town is a posh ski area, many hotels, motels, and kitschy B & B's, and dozens of overpriced restaurants and schlocky art galleries surrounded by vast tracts of BLM and national forest land right out of an Ansel Adams photograph. The more genuine side of our village includes three pawn shops that sell storyteller dolls *and* assault weapons; two county mud pits for amateur tractor pulls; friendly clerks at the post office; and Aaron Osborne's Read & Feed Pre-Owned Book Emporium, my refuge from the smarm. Breathless, I dashed into that venue twenty minutes late still unable to exit A-fib. Aaron, a large hulking fellow, roared, "The Titanic arrives!" Shirley, his nearly blind assistant, hugged me raptly almost tipping me over. Sally said, "Qué pasó? You're all pale. *Oh no here we go again.*" The twenty-five impatient audience members conferred a standing ovation except for Roberto Salazar who catcalled, "Where's the beard? Where's the guitar?" John Wayne Dahmer, the black Persian tomcat dozing beside the computer monitor at the register, never woke up.

"I was about to notify the police and file a missing persons," Aaron said.

I asked him, "Can I use the office and put my feet up for thirty seconds? My heart is having a senior moment."

"Yeah, sure, go for it."

"Wait a minute! Stop this show—he's killing himself," Sally protested. "He's no good to me as a cadaver."

"It's okay, I'll be right back," I told the multitudes. "I need to flush a fetus down the toilet."

Roberto Salazar cried, "Come back, little Sheba!"

Roberto is a good guy who used to be my favorite fishing buddy. And we hunted grouse together every September in the plush mountains southeast of town. We had a ball. Our most fun was driving his jalopy truck out of the hills at night on narrow dirt roads drinking bourbon and

Coke while singing Tex-Mex tunes in English and Spanish. Then Roberto lost his right leg below the knee in an automobile accident. He wasn't driving a car but lying prone underneath one in his driveway futzing with the stabilizer bar when the hydraulic jack collapsed and his leg was crushed. I never understood the details. Since then we've often met at El Patio to drink beer and tequila shooters during important sporting events on their widescreen TV. I can speak Spanish after a fashion—it's one of my plus points—and Roberto humors me as I fracture the lingo. I have to say Aaron and Roberto are my best friends. Sally refuses to converse with me in Spanish because she *knows* all Anglos are illiterate in her natal tongue. It's a case of reverse racism, I believe. Maybe I should hire a lawyer.

In Aaron's office I drank half a bottle of water, lay on my back on the concrete floor, and hooked my heels up over the edge of his desk. Same old, same old, my heart has been weird for a while. I'll admit I was a trifle scared, however. Remember: *Sixty-five is not thirty-five, hotshot.* And, denied sufficient oxygen, the corpuscles of my wretched body were excreting pre-epileptic nausea enzymes and tinnitus buzzed loudly in both ears. Sally looked ravishing in a low-cut lavender blouse, lemon-yellow slacks, and pink sandals. The owners hovered, squinting at me who suddenly had begun to picture myself dead, swollen and noisome on the rug by my bed with many bumpy clumps of blowfly larvae undulating beneath my rotting skin. Cookie and Carlos were standing over my corpse plaintively meowing for their seafood Friskies. I understand nobody lives forever, yet I still don't want to die like that, not now, or at least not before I achieve the unblemished summit of Spoon Mountain with my kids and do my little dance of exaltation on probably the only spot of earth left in our county devoid of the human stain. Nor do I want to die before my granddaughter Lizzy has a chance to imprint me on her budding brain. She calls me "Poppy" and likes me to read her Slinky Malinki books when we have a rare playdate when I visit the Capital City. Lizzy is way too old for Slinky Malinki, but he is one of our rituals. And we love our rituals. Lizzy lets the rats out of their cage and they crawl all over us licking sweat off our earlobes and my Adam's apple while I'm reading aloud. Wynken, Blynken, and Nod. Lizzy juggles the rats as if they were hacky sacks. The Siamese fighting fish, Angelina Aguilera, watches us from under a bubble nest in his goldfish bowl on the windowsill. Sometimes Lizzy gets up and does her jump rope tricks while I'm reading to her. She can listen to Slinky Malinki and do Mad Dog 360s or Shelly Behind the Knees never missing a beat. If I stop reading to concentrate on the speed of her rope and the intricacy of her coordination she'll chant:

Baby baby in the tub,
Mama forgot to put in the plug.
Oh what sorrow! Oh what pain!
There goes baby down the drain!

When I was young I could never jump rope like Lizzy. She's a whiz kid, a professional. Her school team has been featured on Channel 7's "What's Up?" segment. And Lizzy is so smart I believe she already spends half her time at school in a computer pod doing algorithms, and she's not even eight years old. It's a gifted class. But Miranda won't let her skip a grade.

I need to know Lizzy better and vice versa before I call it quits. I've already screwed up royally with Miranda and Ben, but Lizzy is a clean slate. We are in cahoots. There's *hope.*

Aaron said, "Are you okay? Should we call an ambulance? Do you want a cookie?"

"What are you talking about, a cookie?" Sally protested. "Are you nuts? His cholesterol is already over 200. He's a walking time bomb."

And the cookies Aaron had on a huge paper platter would have tripped the ignition switch on that time bomb for sure. They were chocolate chip numbers imbedded with chopped gummy bears and Jujyfruits baked across town at Bob's Diner where the food is crude but the topless dumpsters in back turn me on because they are raven magnets. Now you know. In fact, off and on for years I have stopped by Bob's on late afternoons to watch those big black birds wrangle garbage and I've also talked with them to keep my hand in. Recently, however, I've accelerated my visits. They have become part of my psychological preparation for Spoon Mountain. Back to nature. I want to visualize the wild before I reenter the wild. Sounds hookie-mookie? Perhaps. But my idea of hookie-mookie is, like, getting a colonic from a space cadet who's chanting verses of the Bhagavad Gita while my shit tumbles out through a clear plastic tube into a 30-gallon holding tank full of rose petals. *That's* hookie-mookie.

Aaron said, "He looks awful."

Sally pleaded, "Baby, let me take you home, I'll make chicken soup, this isn't worth it. You're crazy to think about climbing Spoon Mountain on your birthday. Take a rain check and spend it with me. I'll dress up in Frederick's of Hollywood."

Shirley said, "He couldn't manage a ladder to my attic let alone Spoon Mountain on his birthday."

Oh yeah? "How much do you want to bet?" I righted myself, losing my balance, and dived headfirst into the wall, staggering backward surrounded by cuckoos, dust briffits, and twirling spurls.

"A million bucks," Sally wagered. "This is your idea of 'kicking back and mellowing out?'" To Shirley she complained, "Ever since he decided to scale that mountain I can't get through to him at all. He's breaking my heart. I'm losing him even though I never had him in the first place. And I can't say I'm being betrayed because he has always refused to sign on the line."

"Te quiero," I said.

"You love everybody," she replied. "Receiving a 'Te quiero' from you is like getting a wolf whistle from a drunken plumber."

Ferociously, fighting away tears of frustration, I tore open my knapsack, extracted the ratty beard, hooked it on despite a broken tong, buttoned up my grubby Civil War jacket, took a puff off the asthma inhaler, and adopted my booming Walt Whitman persona as I stumbled out front prepared to recite from *Song of Myself*. Walt is one of my alter egos whenever I get bored with reading from my own work. Instead of rhymes by The Good Gray Poet, however, a bunch of banal, chirpy words issued at an almost falsetto pitch from my constricted gullet:

"Hi there everyone, thanks for your marvelous patience. You folks are angels. I'm sorry I was late but guess what? In eight days I'm going to be sixty-five years old and to celebrate I intend to fulfill a decades-old promise to my children by climbing a pretty tall mountain where I expect I'll find—"

And that's when Don the Man lunged through the Read & Feed front doorway swinging a baseball bat. The golem arrives in all its glory. John Wayne Dahmer went flying when the bat crashed against the cash register. Blind Shirley shrieked, Aaron cried "*Wait a minute!*," and audience members scattered like a school of shrimp hit by a hungry grouper. More or less used to these scenes, Sally glommed onto the nearest weapon (a ceramic Mexican vase holding fresh cut zinnias) just as the baseball bat met (and demolished) my lectern (*and* my right forearm raised to deflect the blow)—"Suck on this, you infidel!" Don shouted—and she beaned her ex-hubby with the vase as Aaron and another patron, Gilbert Romero, struck Don with metal folding chairs and he barged into a mobile bookrack that fell with an operatic crash. Aaron and Gilbert Romero landed on top of him while Sally bapped 911 on her cell phone and bleated "*Hurry up!*" at the cops. Roberto Salazar joined the pileup wielding his belt, which he wrapped twice around Don's wrists yanked behind his back in the expert fashion of a seasoned calf roper. By the time Philip Martínez and Eric Thompson arrived Don had been substantially subdued, although he continued snarling random obscenities related to his ex-wife's "puta infidelities."

"Lock him up and throw away the key!" Sally cried as they hustled her ex out to the paddy wagon.

Me? I sat in a corner holding my fractured arm, cursing the fact that I was still one week shy of Medicare, hence uninsured.

Then I vomited.

Fourteen

Miranda was appalled. She was on her cell phone stuck in line at an ATM machine. "What were you doing to him, Johnny? Screwing his wife? Calling him a right-wing dirtbag in public? Giving his children copies of the latest hick-lit novel you published? And who's Sally? The last I heard your girlfriend was Rowena."

"They've been divorced for years," I said. A lightweight fiberglass cast extended from an inch below my right elbow to the main knuckles of my hand protecting the reset ulna. Sally had signed it *Te quiero, güero*; Aaron had scribbled *Spoon Mt. or Bust* (then he doubled my hundred dollar reading fee and I almost kissed him).

"But Don is a volatile misfit on a restraining order," I elaborated. "I don't know what happened or why."

"Like you didn't know what happened or why the day you hit on that starlet, Michelle Grainger, when they were shooting *The Lucky Underdogs*? And her boyfriend, the 'volatile misfit' from the Arena Football League, attacked you with a tennis racket? And that humiliating photograph was in *People* magazine the week I graduated from nursing school?"

"I didn't hit on Michelle," I protested, abashed at my

own pathos. I've had some tacky things happen in life that I'm not proud of, mostly thanks to working on films. There is an aura of naughty behavior that swirls around making a movie and even writers are allowed to scramble for the crumbs discarded from above. I once enjoyed a superb hand job under the Throne Table at Ma Maison while our host, Jack Lemmon, was conferring with the sommelier. My second wife initiated divorce proceedings after she answered the phone one midnight and a continuity girl from the Valley buzzed on crank asked her for "Mr. Forever."

"She hit on me," I elaborated. "However those days are long gone, ancient history. Lanoxin has usurped my testosterone. I'm almost a eunuch, anymore."

Miranda scoffed, "Nobody's a eunuch anymore, Dad, give me a break. There's more pills on the market for male enhancement than there are stars in the universe. Centenarians are fathering *triplets*. Eighty-year-old women have kids in vitro. Speaking of which, are you taking those vitamins I sent?"

"Every morning and every night without fail," I assured her.

"You're lying. I can hear it in your voice."

"No I'm not. Give me a break."

"What about that stew Jamie and Ben brought over? Do you like it?"

"Yes, I love the stuff. Sometimes I dump it over steaming brown rice for supper. And for breakfast I often fry the leftovers and fashion a burrito with a tortilla. Maybe I sprinkle on a dab of Tabasco for extra flavor."

Miranda said, "I can't stand it. Your voice is so dripping

with mendacity. I know you chucked all those containers into the garbage even before Ben's truck was out of the driveway, didn't you?"

"Are you kidding? *Jesus.* Ye of so little faith."

"I bought a bunch of GU packets for our trip up that mountain," she said. "Are you climbing Tecolote Hill every day to get in shape? You better be if you know what's good for you. Are you drinking lots of water?"

"Absolutely. What do you take me for, a slacker? I'm an athlete and this is a serious endeavor."

"You used to be an athlete, Dad, before three wives and fifteen girlfriends, twenty years of Hollywood, asthma and heart problems, alcohol and horrible eating habits, arthritis, extreme stress, and chronic lack of sleep cut you down to the size of a crippled church mouse."

"Very funny, Miranda. We are going to climb that mountain *now* before the Floresta shuts down the national forest because of fire danger."

"You think you're immortal but you're not," she insisted. "Just because you've dodged so many bullets in the past doesn't mean that the next one hasn't got your name on it."

I said, "Not being afraid of dying is paramount to human liberation."

Whatever *that* means. I've always been prone to ersatz philosophical pronouncements, I am facile with meaningless aphorisms. Blame my silver tongue. All my life I have projected more false bravado than a gaggle of teenage boys on a diving board at a public swimming pool. "Throw out the bums!" "Vote Socialist!" "Free Huey Newton!" Truth is, though, I am deathly afraid of my own shadow. Like, for instance, right now. I prefer that nobody, least of all my children, knows that. So I am a brazen poseur. One must pretend to be confident and seething with vitality even if riddled by bad health and paranoia. I suspect Miranda intuits I'm just another petrified Caspar Milquetoast underneath. Often I feel so trapped in my sardonic repartee with Miranda I want to kill myself. If only we had a different formula for communication that was more genteel and not so insult oriented. On the other hand I wish I could simply *communicate* with Ben. How is immaterial. Yet I don't know how. For whatever reasons we are mostly mute with each other. I don't know anything *real* about his life. I know more about my cats Cookie and Carlos than I do about my own children. How skewed is that?

Miranda said, "Bueno, Dad, let's drop the mindless banter for a moment so I can put it to you straight for once. Time out, please. Nobody is not afraid of dying, not me, not Ben, not even you. And the fact is I'm worried about you. I'm being serious for a change so don't brush me off, okay?"

There was an opening, a rare one between us, so why didn't I take it? That is a sixty-four-thousand-dollar question and I don't know how to answer it. My life seems to be guided by a hodgepodge of knee-jerk reactions antithetical to what I actually feel in my heart. It's a dilemma.

"Okay, Mandy," I said. "Thanks sweetie. It's always good to chew the fat with you. Bye-bye."

Fifteen

Miranda was right, however: I *used* to be an athlete. Yet I was a pretty good athlete for a while. During prep school back in Connecticut I played first-string football, I was captain of the hockey team, I ran the mile and low hurdles for track. In college I quit football and started cross-country, became captain of the hockey team again, and ran the low hurdles come spring. After college I stayed in shape. When we were New Yorkers I jogged daily over to the East River and ran up and down the exercise walkway beside the Jacob Riis housing projects. Not all communists are pallid intellectuals wearing rimless spectacles slumped over in dank basements under a single light bulb memorizing the collected works of Kim Il-sung.

After moving west I took up hunting and fishing and hiking and playing tennis well enough to win the B tournament at our rinky-dink local park. I was coordinated. "Call me Baryshnikov," I joked. I was serious. As soon as Ben and Miranda were old enough I helped coach them in Little League and Youth Soccer so they could take up where the old man left off.

Ben did okay at Little League but was intimidated by the ferociousness of team competition. He switched to a more solitary sport, BMX bike racing. Picture this huge kid on a tiny bike who racked up dozens of trophies. In high school he built himself a mountain bike and disappeared into the hills. No more competition for Ben. He much preferred to pedal off into the countryside by himself. He carried his fanny pack with the insulin, the needles, a glucometer, and energy bars in case of emergency. I never knew if he was frightened. He did not let on. Nowadays he has an insulin pump. Progress is our most important product.

Miranda loved competition. She became a fierce high school basketball player down in the Capital City. Her adamant ways scared me. I drove south for some of her games. Summers, we shot baskets in our old driveway before I lost the house during my second divorce. The house on Upper Ranchitos Road that went to "Dolly Parton." It was a ramshackle adobe with a leaky roof, prehistoric rusted plumbing, driveway potholes deeper than bomb craters, and a tilting outhouse, but it had character. Miranda and I rigged up a spotlight so we could play H-O-R-S-E in the driveway at midnight and Miranda always beat me, I did not stand a chance. Basketball was never my cup of tea anyway, there's too much scoring and the refs control the finish of every game. Let 'em play, I say. Junior year Miranda was point guard on a team that lost the state championship by a single bucket in the second overtime. When I attempted to console her afterward she interrupted me: "Oh get a life, Dad, spare me your childish homilies." Then she laughed bitterly and said, "Wait'll next year." And she quoted Scarlett O'Hara: "After all, tomorrow is another day."

That is Miranda's all-time favorite saying. As Ben is a

starship *Enterprise* freak even today, Miranda was a *Gone with the Wind* Trekkie. She knew the entire movie by heart. A few lines she beat into my suffering brain are: "Fiddle dee dee, war war war, I get so bored I could scream." "As God is my witness they're not going to lick me, I'm going to live through this and when it's all over I'll never be hungry again." "Great balls of fire, don't bother me anymore and don't call me sugar."

Miranda named our Upper Ranchitos outhouse "Tara." "I loved that outhouse," she enthuses even today. "I remember the hummingbirds that came to the hollyhocks beside Tara whenever I took a poop."

Ben has never criticized me for losing that house in my second divorce. Miranda has *always* criticized me for losing it. To hear her talk you would think the house was a castle on a cloud framed by a rainbow halo like Disneyland. Not so. Sally would have listed it as "a great fixer-upper," or "a fabulous starter home." Translation: "Buy this derelict, then hire a bulldozer to flatten it and begin again from scratch." Miranda's comeback? "Remember when we skated on the irrigation ditch? And played volleyball in the front field? And what about Ben's pigeons, and the haystack beside the woodpile, and our chickens that laid all those eggs?"

One fateful summer I commenced a relationship with a daffy amazon named Tammy Pierce who had three children of her own, all of whom belonged in a juvenile psychiatric lockdown. Miranda hated them and Ben was required by her to hate them also although Ben hated nobody. He felt sorry for the Pierce kids and would talk to them if Tammy brought them over. One had a cleft palate.

Another was an Indigo child. Miranda locked herself in the bathroom and soaked in the tub reading *MAD* magazines until they were gone.

Twice a week Tammy brought us over a platter of deep-fried chicken drumsticks or a sweet potato pie or two dozen delicious Toll House cookies that I devoured hungrily while Miranda boycotted the evil food from evil Tammy. Ben avoided the cookies for health reasons. At the time I thought Miranda's surliness was funny and chalked it up to her adolescent immaturity. Which only goes to show that I was clueless. I suspect that my whole life I have been clueless even though people used to tell me my books were full of "profound insights into the human heart and into the human condition" (*St. Louis Post-Dispatch*, October 27, 1983). Reviewers have not been quite as charitable with my later oeuvre, which one arrogant blowhard for the NYTBR summed up as "Much ado about nothing." You can't win 'em all.

Sad to say, Tammy Pierce is the woman Miranda dubbed "Dolly Parton." Tammy was very curvaceous and her attire ran a gamut from low-cut Lycra jerseys to skintight spandex pedal pushers and back again. I still don't know how she pulled it off; I was dazed because my inner Shallow Guy was controlling the narrative. But wait. Tammy had an undergraduate degree in sociology from Ohio State and a master's in business administration from Iowa. When I met her she was running a successful catering operation that specialized in funeral receptions. Cherry tarts and quince empanaditas to honor the dearly departed. My town attracts people like her. But that's not all. Tammy was a liberal Democrat who helped me organize a protest against grand jury abuse. We were both members of the local U.S.-China Peoples' Friendship Association. During her younger days she had gone on *two* Venceremos Brigades to cut sugarcane in Cuba. To boot, she had read *all* my books and could recite by heart a few long passages from several of them. And the film version of *The Lucky Underdogs* was her favorite movie; she'd watched it twenty-one times.

In short, Tammy was everything I had always fantasized about but was afraid to ask for. So we married and shortly thereafter my Upper Ranchitos house devolved to that girl in the divorce proceedings. "Mr. Forever," remember? Behind every irresistible starlet attached to a Shallow Guy there's always an X-rated little Machiavelli who can lead you by the hand through Fodor's Official Divorce and Property Settlement Manual. I was her third victim and, obviously, deserved what I got. The arc is way more complex than that but why dwell on the gory details? My friend Roberto Salazar says, "You came, you saw, you were conquered. End of story. Exeunt omnes, pursued by a bear."

Her senior year in high school Miranda's basketball team walloped the gang they'd lost to the previous year, and they went on to demolish their opponent in the championship game. Miranda still keeps her trophy on the faux fireplace mantle in the home she shares with Michael and Lizzy. Her mother and I got drunk celebrating and wound up in bed, a serious mistake though predictable. It's in the blood. Just because my first ex is a respected divorce lawyer does not mean she's stable. Cut me some slack.

Ben attended all of Miranda's high school games but never said a word afterward. It wasn't his style to gush out congratulations. He smiled and nodded his head at her and kept to the background while everyone else noisily rehashed the contest. Miranda knew that Ben had been in attendance, though. He did not have to say anything. "Ben always has my back, Dad, I can count on him. He's not like you. He is steadfast. He's my Mount Everest."

"What am I?" I foolishly asked.

"You're my Mount St. Helens," she replied.

Sad to say, I am not that much of an athlete anymore. I have zero coordination. During my endocarditis bout while hitched to Wife #3 the IV antibiotic treatment with gentamicin blew out my inner ears so that my balance now depends exclusively on eyesight. When I walk I see the world like a handheld movie camera. Everything bounces. That's called oscillopsia. I cannot hit a tennis ball and ice skating is out of the question. If I try to dance with Sally at the Sagebrush Inn I stumble sideways into the band's drummer during his solos. About all I can do is hike using a couple of poles for equilibrium. These days nobody calls me Baryshnikov. However, that doesn't mean I can't climb to the top of Spoon Mountain, quite the contrary: I am riddled from toes to nose with fortitude. Nobody impugns my grit, pluck, and spunk. Despite appearances to the contrary, I'm a mensch.

Just ask me.

Sixteen

Ben said, "I'm sorry you are hurt, Pop." He was embarrassed for me. I don't blame him. Ben has never commented to me about the unhappy consequences of my amorous liaisons. I have to believe they leave him speechless.

"Thanks, Ben. I appreciate your concern."

"Is there anything I can do for you?" he asked. "When I get off work I could go to the store."

"I don't think so. Everything is copacetic."

"I'm glad," Ben said. "I'm glad you're okay. I'm glad the bat didn't hit your head." It's not easy for him to show overt emotion. When I asked him to scribble something on my cast he wrote *Best Wishes, Ben.*

"Me too," I said. "Thanks, Ben."

"You're welcome, Pop."

"Okay. Thanks for stopping by."

"No problem."

Ben was hunched behind the wheel of his pickup truck in my driveway. Even though the truck is a large Toyota, he still seems way too big for the roomy cab. Maybe that is simply his forceful presence. Ben's hands are "ginormous" (as my granddaughter Lizzy would say). Half the fingernails have blood blisters under them from errant hammer blows. Ben is a bona fide nail pounder. His current project is building the swimming pool addition at the new rec center on the highway bypass. He is a foreman on the job.

Cujo was crouched in the Toyota bed alertly scoping my yard for any sign of Cookie or Carlos. If he had spotted either of them he would have become airborne headed directly for my kitty (or kitties), his bared teeth glistening and saliva strands slobbering rearward past his dewlaps as he chased after her (or him) with murder on his pea-sized canine brain. Whenever Cookie and Carlos hear Ben's truck approaching along Valverde Street they whiz up an elm tree in one second flat or flee indoors to the refuge of my bedroom closet where Cujo can't pursue them since his muscle-bound body won't magically vaporize itself to whoosh through the cat door as if in a *Tom and Jerry* cartoon.

My granddaughter Lizzy loves *Tom and Jerry*, consequently so do I. I have six DVDs of those goofy old shows that I've purchased over the years. They are very violent, also borderline racist, although Whoopi Goldberg says they are cool as long as you view them within a historical context that is now passé. What the cartoons have going for them is they are clever, well drawn, and riotously funny. Lizzy and I guffaw whenever Tom, the idiot conniving cat, splats against a tree trunk full-bore driving his tongue, teeth, and eyeballs back through his brains or Jerry, the obnoxious trickster mouse, is squashed into the ground when Tom drops an anvil onto him. The sight gags are horrendous and hilarious, right up Lizzy's and my alleys. On the rare occasions that Lizzy visits me at my house we pop in one of those DVDs the minute Michael and Miranda aren't looking. "By all means, you guys should go out for a libation at El Patio," Lizzy and I chime in unison to her parents, encouraging them to leave home so we mice can play our *Tom and Jerry* DVDs. "We'll hold down this fort," we assure them. And indeed we will.

"Well, call me if you need anything," Ben said. "I'll come right over. Do you remember my cell phone number?"

"Yes, thank you. I promise. Thank you again." Ben and I can be horrendously polite to each other. That drives me crazy. If Miranda is my Don Rickles, Ben is my Atticus Finch. Understand, I'm not criticizing. Things could be a lot worse.

"Okay," Ben said. He started his truck. "Don't forget."

"I won't, I'm an elephant."

Ben rarely reacts to my agile bon mots. He has heard enough of them to last a lifetime.

"I'll see you, then," Ben said.

"Not if I see you first," I said. That's another joke. I am never sure if Ben gets it although I've used that quip on him since he was three years old. My son is not as flatline as his girlfriend Jamie when it comes to a sense of humor, yet I would not accuse him of being a sitcom laugh track, either. Ben doesn't read my books because detailed sex scenes give him a nervous stomach. They're annoying. About *The Lucky Underdogs* movie he said, "It was pretty funny, Pop." He only saw the picture once and Jamie said he fell asleep halfway through. The lad works hard at his job.

Ben reached out his window and lightly touched me

on the shoulder. With him that's what passes for profound emotion. I was grateful.

He drove off cautiously, checking both ways at the top of my driveway before turning onto Valverde Street. Ben invariably checks both ways. He has never been in an accident. That could be why he's tarried so long asking Jamie to marry him. Ben needs to be sure the way lies safe in all directions. Twice I've heard Jamie grumble about Ben's extended marital hesitation . . . in a whisper. You had better believe Jamie is behind her man 1,000 percent.

Myself on the other hand? I have had seven auto accidents over my long career, nothing too serious, although I once put my front teeth through my tongue by banging my chin against the steering wheel when I drove a VW Bus off Interstate 70 by mistake late at night near Columbus, Ohio. Too, eight years ago, fleeing from a bad situation, I managed to roll my Dodge Shadow over three times into a shallow creek where I almost drowned because I was unable to unbuckle my seat belt from an upside-down position. How did I roll over into a creek? One, I wasn't paying attention. Two, there was a patch of ice on the road. Three, Kepler's Third Law of Motion according to Miranda applied. In my world there is usually a patch of ice on the road. If it isn't actual ice it is metaphorical ice, right? We could say that Don the Man is a patch of ice on my road, or my heart condition is, or Sally Trevino, or even Spoon Mountain if we're covering all bases here. I hope I'm not headed for accident number eight, however. Nobody should push their luck that far, not even me.

Seventeen

Two days after the Read & Feed fiasco, Sally came over to apologize for Don the Man by hauling my ashes. But she required it to be special and exotic, not a cursory hump made drabber by my dour pad. So off we went in her silver Isuzu Trooper to an adobe trophy McMansion on Blueberry Hill, the second home for a pair of decadent faith-based entrepreneurs from Texas. Sally had the keys. "He's in oil and gas; she runs a Fort Worth gallery. They attend church at their bank on Sundays. This humble joint is on the block because they decided to switch their vacation operation to San Miguel de Allende. They also own a condo on Maui and a cottage on Martha's Vineyard. The crime rate here finally discouraged them and a starving bear ate their cairn terrier. This house has been burglarized three times over the last eighteen months and tagged by gangbangers twice. God hates the rich."

Talk about conspicuous space and ostentation. It made me want to weep. This was her idea of romance? Cathedral ceilings were fourteen feet high, the vigas massive, blond, beautiful. Sunlight streamed in through wide floor-to-ceiling thermal-paned windows. The floors were polished oaken slats or Mexican tile with radiant heating underneath. You could have played soccer in the living room watched by five hundred fans. There were ornate Persian rugs, a wide-screen TV, a sophisticated stereo system. A thousand mint-condition hardback first editions stocked library shelves. The kitchen had copper pans and iron kettles hanging off pegs, a professional chef's vainglorious paradise. All told it was a spotless operation, from the skylights to the well-tended plants nurtured by a weekly garden service that met seasonal landscaping needs and also took care of the swimming pool, the outdoor Jacuzzi, the indoor hot tub, and the tanning salon.

A sultan-sized four-poster sleeping barge ruled the master bedroom. It had a thick quilt the color of mountain bluebirds. The view through panoramic windows comprised the haze-dimmed Sangre de Cristo range from Arroyo Verde to Boulder Peak casting shadows across our town. Spoon Mountain occupied the exact middle of the smoggy picture—flanked by Gavilán and Cabrito Peaks— its nipple-shaped nub of a summit sloping gently south along a ridge to the Catherine Lake Overlook. The smog had wafted up from two fires south of the Capital City and from a monster blaze over in Arizona, par for the summer course. "Ladies and gentlemen: Cruise the colorful Southwest in your Winnebago Braves admiring the estival flames of Hades. Feed honey-roasted cashews to the malnourished bears. Take a dehydrated chipmunk to lunch."

I'll admit I was stunned by the difference between this baroque showcase castle and my own diminutive shanty, which is three tiny rooms measuring seven hundred square feet full of paperback books, stacks of manuscripts and unanswered mail, and other generic rubble.

"How much are they asking for this monstrosity?" I asked.

"A million eight hundred thousand. And they'll get it, too."

"Fuck them. Fuck those—"

"I am *soooo* sorry about Don the Man," Sally interrupted, kissing me passionately. She can't stand it when I fly off the handle on a political tangent and usually cuts me off by saying, "Save it for election day, Boris." She doesn't read my books either because, "All your male characters have deformed libidos and all your female characters have boob jobs and abrasive personalities." Sally thinks that's tacky.

"I had no idea Don would actually attack you," she continued. "I was only joking about telling him we were lovers to help you commit suicide. I never in a million years—"

"That's okay," I whispered. "It was bound to happen sooner or later."

Sally slid down my torso, kneeling between my legs, and unzipped my fly and pried out the docile iguana, engulfing it between her painted lips with an infinitely sexy tenderness giving me dreamy head like a Renaissance artist painting the summer clouds above Holland. Physically, I'm no porn star but in my experience any woman able to deep-throat me is an exceptional sex partner. Sally does not have a gag reflex. "I was born this way," she brags. "It's a gift from God."

My pal Roberto Salazar introduced us when Sally asked him to ask me if I would give the keynote address at a conference of western realtors in Cheyenne, Wyoming, a year ago last April. Their theme was Responsible Property Marketing. "There'll be two hundred drunk Republicans wearing Stetson cowboy hats, snakehide Lucchese boots, and double-knit golf slacks," Sally explained at our first meeting. "They'll give you a thousand dollars and we can drive up in my car."

You would be amazed at how many different kinds of conferences will hire me because of *The Lucky Underdogs*. Often they run that feel-good film in advance to soften up my audience. It's a "charming populist comedy" masquerading as relevant commentary. "Saccharine socialism with an occasional chuckle," hooted the *New York Times*. Water off my back. I give great speech, slanted toward whomever (I'm a chameleon, call me Zelig), oozing with witticisms and plenty of self-deprecating humor. I'm a cross between Will Rogers and Malcolm X. People can ignore my political barbs if they want because my jesting is "all in fun." Laugh and the world laughs with you (you decadent capitalist cocksuckers!). And I am not proud, I will take the money and run because I need it to stave off my repo men. Even Karl Marx had to feed his children.

That was a great trip. We wound up skinny-dipping in the motel swimming pool at midnight during an April snowfall. Then we knocked Sally's motel room for a loop with our energetic hijinks. Yes, I had brought along a few blue pills just in case because you rarely get a second chance to make a first impression.

"Love me tender, Elvis," Sally whispered into my ear. "I'm all shook up. Ándale, nene. *Make me happy.*"

By the time we reached the state line on our return journey I was almost ready to ask for her hand in marriage. Almost. A guy like me can only go to the well so often. And yet—

Dreedle eep bleep tweet.

The call to Sally was from Chip. "Don't go away," she murmured to me, then explained to Chip: "Chip, it's a commercial building in an attractive location. It can easily be divided into four or five spaces with at least two rentable apartments or more if you wanted. Because of the photo lab in there six years ago tests will have to be done to make sure there's no toxic residue, you can't avoid that. Irregardless, given the possible future earnings and the great location, two and a quarter is a weak listing. I wouldn't commence with anything lower than two-fifty. If you're willing to carry the paper or wind up having to carry it you can ask for more. I'd stake my license on it. Ciao, bello."

But I couldn't get back into it, even with half a pill. I was as wilted as Free Willy's dorsal fin. Now and again, when I listen to Sally talking real estate, I feel totally demoralized. Like, how could I ever hang out at length with a person who sells real estate even though I seem to be enamored of a person who sells real estate? Just don't tell her, please, I don't want to declare myself yet, at least not for reals, if you know what I mean. "For reals," I'm afraid, would take place in the Catholic church before Father Rumaldo and his eight octogenarian Rosary Girls, a fate worse than death. But you know what another problem is? Sally has Alex, Zachary, and Jason and those boys freak me out.

Alex is six feet tall, he wears Gucci earrings, and, when he's decorated with mascara and lipstick, he could be an actor from the movies *Beetlejuice* or *Men in Black*. Zachary is over six feet and has been to jail three times for deliberately crashing his skateboard into obnoxious tourists on the Plaza. Jason is a shrimp, scarcely taller than Sally, yet a great athlete on both the football and wrestling teams. His problem, aside from a lack of driving skills? He stutters badly. For that reason he is pathologically shy and takes special ed classes in high school.

How could I ever be their stepfather? I must say, though, that Sally is not intimidated by her sons. Sure, she complains—who wouldn't? They're teenagers. They steal CDs, they crash cars, they've watched *Kill Bill* once a week for three years. No matter. Sally forces them to love and respect each other and herself. I don't know how she does it. They almost never talk back to her. She communicates with them on their level. She pays attention to their schoolwork, always ragging them about it. They will all finish high school because Sally will *will* them to finish high school. Alex won't get away with quitting his senior year, I promise. Defying his mother on that issue is not an option, his psycho dad to the contrary notwithstanding.

And this might astound the casual observer. Alex and his brothers help out at home. Yes they do. They keep their rooms fairly neat. They don't put their boat-sized feet up on the furniture. Sally does not run their dirty laundry through the washing machine twice a week after work, the boys wash their own duds and hang them on the outside line to dry. Sally also attends speech therapy with Jason.

She attends all his football games and wrestling matches. She supported a fashion show that Alex produced at the high school, threatening to keelhaul Don the Man if he lifted a finger to queer it. Zachary bangs the snare drum in band and practices at home without driving the rest of them crazy. That is Sally's stamp.

What's more, my girlfriend goes overboard to provide her three bottomless pits with decent healthy meals. I mentioned that earlier. When they are with Don the Man those boys eat Egg McMuffins for breakfast, lunch, and dinner. None of the kids smoke cigarettes, that is one of Sally's taboos. Do they puff on marijuana because their mother likes a toke to relax? No they do not. How did she accomplish that? Beats me. I'm guessing that Alex, Zachary, and Jason feel safe with Sally. Despite her wayward adventures with men and the zanier aspects of her job, Sally is solid for her children, unlike their father whose parenting philosophy could be stashed in the brain of a nematode worm. The boys trust their mom because they can depend on her. I could not say that about my own kids re their dad, could I?

Bottom line? So. What. It remains a fact: Sally's boys are another glitch in my relationship with her. I must keep a distance from them, hence from her. That confuses me. I feel lonely. Maybe the only person on earth who truly loves me (and whom I truly love in return) is my granddaughter Lizzy. She's not old enough to know better. In her eyes I'm not loaded down with baggage. In Sally's eyes I must come across like a redcap at O'Hare International Airport tagging after a family of Saudi royals returning to Riyadh after an extended shopping trip in America. To hang with me my girlfriend has more courage than a mongoose and if I lose her I am doomed. When I commence ruminating along these lines I remind myself: "Chill, take three steps backward, you've done enough damage in your life."

On other occasions when I listen to Sally talking real estate I am rendered aghast by hideous visions of what we are doing to the earth where I see Japanese factory boats drenched in whale blood or dead camels decomposing on a salt desert where the Aral Sea used to be. And suddenly I feel breathless. Can we *ever* fulfill the long-suppressed expectations of our genes? The odds are growing so much longer against. Then I think about Yahoos like Don the Man and I can't even muster tepid wrath against them because they are not the problem, they're powerless, mere fragments of collateral damage, why blame the victims? Given my druthers I'd set Don free from the county jail, he deserves another chance and I don't want him for my enemy. Then reward me, please, for being magnanimous. I would sincerely appreciate a gold star on my forehead *before* I get to heaven. They gave Gorbachev a Nobel Peace Prize, why not me?

"What's wrong, mi alma?" Sally asked, cupping the poor palomita between her delicate palms like a flickering votive candle. "I've offended your lefty snobbism once again by interrupting our idyll to sell a piece of property to pay my rent, feed my children, and buy lingerie that turns you on?" She glanced up at my doleful eyes and, reacting to their gaze, turned her head to look out the picture window toward the smoky landscape I was fixated upon.

"Oh I see," she said, drawing away from me and buttoning up her blouse. "I should have known." Sally folded her arms and regarded me with almost bored disappointment. "Once again that mountain is destroying our so-called relationship."

Eighteen

That mountain? I don't think so, girlfriend. I began my mountain climbing career shortly after we moved to the Southwest from New York in 1969, decades before Sally entered the picture. At first I reconnoitered the lower elevations, fishing small rivers that trickled from spruce, Douglas fir, and aspen forests down into the ponderosa belt and finally through piñon and juniper trees to the valley where much water is siphoned off by irrigation ditches. Throughout the 1970s I creeled a half-dozen native cutthroats each afternoon as well as my limit of brown trout. Due to willows, chokecherries, and alders crowding the stream banks I had to waddle up the middle of the little rivers snapping my line ahead as if from a bow and arrow. The cutthroats are mostly gone today because they perish in the warmer water.

By the 1980s I was forging higher to catch rainbows and stocked cutthroat in small lakes between ten and twelve thousand feet. That's when I introduced Ben and Miranda to Gallegos Lake on camping trips. They were old enough and they loved the mountains. We experienced a handful of splendid summers together in the high country. We sat around campfires toasting marshmallows and singing songs I had taught them. Ben's favorite was "The Streets of Laredo." Miranda preferred "The Kid's Last Fight." We fried up our few trout keepers. Miranda and I caught the fish while Ben meandered away gazing at pikas, yellow-rumped warblers, and bighorn sheep through his binoculars. Ben refused to kill a fish or anything else. Miranda enjoyed cooking but hated eating the trout: "Ugh, they are so *bony!*" So I had to bring along tins of Spam for her meals. On the other hand Ben *loved* eating the trout. Go figure. Protein is nontoxic to diabetics.

Every day I gave them lessons on birds and botany. They learned to identify the melodious tweetings of ruby-crowned kinglets and hermit thrushes. They could tell the difference between adult white-crowned sparrows and first-year juveniles. Ben studied the plants carefully. Miranda acted bored. She craved action, she wanted to explore new places, get to the *top*. "Quit dicking around, let's *go*," was her mantra. "Be patient," I countered. "Life is long. East St. Louis wasn't built in a day."

I wanted my kids to be naturalists, to love the earth from a biocentric point of view. How else can the planet survive? "This is a twisted stalk, you guys. And this is a fringed gentian. And this is a bog gentian. It's also called Swertia. Now let me show you the difference between arnica and groundsel. Arnica has opposite leaves. See? And groundsel has alternate leaves—"

"Okay, okay," Miranda interrupted. "We see. We get the picture. Vámonos."

Ben was in no hurry to conquer mountains. He bent closer, really studying the plants, counting the stamens and pistils, the teeth on each leaf, committing all the details to memory. He was interested and meticulous, not bored stiff like Miranda. He riffled through the guidebook to read about this Jacob's ladder or that Colorado columbine, behavior I encouraged.

That tedious behavior exasperated Miranda. She clicked her tongue impatiently, calling in gray jays who pecked raisins off her fingertips. Organic raisins that I bought at our local health food store. Gray jays will even land on your head if you've got food. They are also called camp robbers and whiskey jacks. I used to feed them during the winters when I walked on snowshoes through spruce trees atop seven feet of snow. Obviously, I don't do that anymore because seven feet of snow would be a miracle. *Three* feet of snow is a miracle. Miranda gave the gray jays names like Algernon or Ashley Wilkes. She rolled her eyes to the sky when I launched one of my chatting sprees with the wild ravens who often dive-bombed us. "You don't know what they're saying, Dad," she insisted. "Yes I do," I replied. "I've been talking with ravens for years."

Of course, on our next outing Ben could not remember the identities of any plants, yet Miranda's recall was Linnaeus redux. "Oh, that's a sickletop lousewort," she tossed off, "and those are early cinquefoils, but these guys are avens, you can tell by the different leaves." Beep! Beep! She left Ben eating her dust. You only had to tell Miranda something once and it became permanently engraved on her memory. She never had to consult a guidebook. Guidebooks bored her. Plants bored her. Birds bored her. Even bighorn sheep bored her because all they ever did was graze or lie around chewing their cuds. "It's like watching paint dry," Miranda said, folding up our spotting scope. I never understood her antipathy because bighorn sheep enthrall me. They are mysterious Ice Age mammals living in a rugged territory devoid of amenities who are beautiful, alert, fragile yet indestructible, always watching the area quietly. They are *regal.*

Miranda was not bored by bear poop. Bear poop excited her. She wanted to see one of the bears up close and personal. "Show me those bruins." There used to be a lot more of them in the mountains before the drought. Nowadays, the bears all hang out down in our town on street corners selling pencils from tin cups and apples for a nickel apiece. Without bears on earth life will be sad indeed.

At home in the Upper Ranchitos house Ben and I sat at the kitchen table pouring over guidebooks after supper while Miranda watched *Honeymooners* reruns or read Judy Blume. She obsessed almost as much on Judy Blume as on *Gone with the Wind.* "Can You Hear Me, God? It's me, Miranda." Ben could not figure out the difference between larkspur and monkshood. Miranda would jeer, "That's so easy it isn't even funny." She never had to study for anything and scored As on all her school tests. Ben killed himself cramming for exams and flunked half of them. On the other half he was lucky to earn a C-.

For a couple of years Miranda tried to help Ben study, but eventually she capitulated, saying: "You're not stupid, Ben, you just have a different kind of brain. That's okay, however. Einstein had a different kind of brain. So does Stephen Hawking."

When Ben was first diagnosed with type 1 diabetes at my house he disliked pricking his finger to get blood, and he abhorred giving himself insulin shots. I was not any more proficient at those tasks. I'm squeamish. Needles make me queasy. So after Ben and Miranda returned from a couple of weeks with their mom in the Capital City learning the drill, Miranda commandeered the operation on my turf. That was difficult for me to accept since she was only nine. *Nine.* Yet she had learned how to count carbs for Ben and suck insulin into his needles and tap up the air bubbles and make the injections painless. She supervised as he wrote the facts in his diary. "Nothing will ever happen to Ben on my watch," she swore. She was adamant. I asked her mother over the phone if I could trust our little girl in this endeavor. "Yes," she said, "Miranda is competent unlike other people we know who shall remain nameless." I have always been an easy target for irritated females.

You could not see Spoon Mountain from Gallegos Lake, it was too far west and blocked by intervening hills. But you could see Gavilán Peak rising from the east side of the lake and the jagged ridgelines and spectacular mountaintops circling the basin around *toward* Spoon Mountain. I forget how old my kids were when Miranda said, "Let's climb Gavilán Peak." Not that old. I remember Ben said, "Are you crazy?" Miranda said, "Last one to the top is a rotten egg."

Our hike to the summit that day was not a breeze. Gavilán Peak is steep. And it is high. At the top you are 13,168 feet above sea level, you are 1,000 feet above tree limit, and 2,500 feet above Gallegos Lake. Bottom line, Gallegos Lake to the crest of Gavilán Peak is a serious vertical challenge. Still, everybody climbs the peak because it's the tallest in our state. That is its charisma. The mountain's flanks are smooth and grassy and the trail is like a highway. The journey must have taken us four hours. Halfway up Miranda realized she had made a mistake but would not admit it. I had no problem, as I've said my heart was healthy in those days. Surprisingly, for a big awkward kid, Ben had no difficulty either. He was born to be a mountain man. The strong silent type.

Obdurate Miranda kept doing it wrong. She would pound eagerly ahead of us in order to lead, then hit a wall and plop down goggle-eyed and gasping. Ben and I would catch up to her, halt, and gaze around thoughtfully at the magnificent landscape. If one of us happened to glance at huffing, puffing Miranda, she growled, "Shut up. Stop looking at me."

When she could breathe again, Miranda jumped up and began racing ahead of us toward the summit until she smacked another wall and collapsed once more.

Eventually, when Ben and I leisurely caught up to her, I said, "You have to pace yourself, Miranda. You can't sprint to the top of a mountain. Don't be a rabbit, be a turtle."

"*You* be a turtle," she grumbled back, and barreled upward pell-mell. When I looked to Ben for an opinion, he shrugged. Ben is not autistic, although you can't prove that beyond a shadow of a doubt.

Hands down, Miranda beat us to the top. Of course, if Ben and I had continued hiking whenever she self-destructed we would have reached our destination two hours ahead of her. At the summit my shell-shocked daughter crumpled to earth with a purple face, puffy cheeks, sweat-drenched hair and a T-shirt that seemed to have been soaked in Gatorade. When her pounding adolescent heart returned to sinus rhythm she announced coolly, "That was a piece of cake."

Ben nodded in agreement.

Me, I was gazing through binoculars a mile west across the alpine bowl to where a now visible Spoon Mountain beckoned me with its dramatic north cirque and massive boulder fields and snow patches even in July. These days there are never snow patches in July. That was my first glimpse of Spoon Mountain. It is not as high nor as intimidating as Gavilán Peak. For that reason no trails lead to the summit and few people bushwhack to the top. Why bother? It's not challenging enough to be in a guidebook. I watched a dozen ravens circling above Spoon Ridge and beneath them I counted twenty-one bighorn rams grazing along the tundra silhouetted against the western horizon.

That placid scene captured my imagination. A friendly little mountain ignored by the adrenaline junkies, what better recommendation? And, if I had been into hokey spirituality, ravens and bighorn sheep would have become my totem animals. So for the next few years I was a Spoon Mountain fanatic, climbing it often with Ben and Miranda until Hollywood, bad food and hard liquor, two more botched marriages and a dozen inappropriate girlfriends plus grave health issues tumbled me off the wagon. You could say that I lost touch with my cognitive ecology. And my glamorous life, so to speak, fell into the toilet as, coincidentally, climate change assaulted the Southwest, drying up grasslands and riddling forests with spruce budworm, then leveling them both with wildfires.

Nineteen

SWISH-PAN to the present day. INTERIOR SHOT. DOLLY IN for a CLOSEUP. I'm sitting at the kitchen table working on my Magnum Opus when there comes a knock on the kitchen door. Cookie jumped off her pillow on the table and ran to hide in the bedroom closet. Carlos prefers to sleep on my bed, it's much closer to the closet refuge. I have not mentioned the Magnum Opus before, which doesn't mean I had not been writing on it every day and night for the past five years. I am a diligent worker bee who refuses to throw in the towel.

The Magnum Opus is a novel, a massive, and, I would like to think, clever satire about pending Armageddon. In it I have resisted the urge to excoriate the ruling class with my usual overwrought bombast. I'm trying instead to recapture the whimsical outrage of *The Lucky Underdogs* without resorting to the goofy eco-porn of my more recent and highly unsuccessful efforts. Too well I recall Arthur Mizener's biography of F. Scott Fitzgerald, *The Far Side of Paradise*, which my English lit peers and I devoured with romantic hunger in college. Thereafter, we all wanted to crack up and croak at forty, having once been famous drunks. Dare I compare myself now to Fitzgerald at the end of his sorrowful days, scribbling away in the Garden of Allah desperately hoping to resurrect his career with *The Last Tycoon*, a novel he never finished? The final picture I wrote for Hollywood was a sequel to *Midnight Express*, that tale of jail in Turkey whose screenplay, written by Oliver Stone, propelled him to power, popularity, and public pontificating. My follow-up script detailed Billy Hayes's frantic escape from gaol and his flight across Asia Minor and Thrace to Greece. Gradually, rewrite after rewrite, polish after polish, tweak after tweak, the movie disintegrated into a parody of male buddy road epics (with guns) that, had it finally been realized (it wasn't), probably would have been released solely as a video game on Xbox, and then only as a footnote to Grand Theft Auto III. That's when I decided to write serious literature again.

At nearly a thousand pages, so far, the manuscript of my Magnum Opus is daunting. There are over fifty characters. I like to think big (hence I usually fail big). Currently, I am slogging through the tenth or twelfth draft, I've lost count. Although the entire project is a muddle I am not discouraged—yet I need to wrap it up, don't I?, before much more time has elapsed. As Hollywood used to say in all its contracts, *Time is of the essence.* And these days I hear Time's wingèd chariot drawing near.

My problem is I never plan out my novels, I usually achieve them through relentless trial and error. I am intellectually disorganized and easily led to dead-end solutions. I don't know what is wrong with my shit detector, it has been on the fritz since kindergarten. My overabundant energy is often trumped by a serious lack of aesthetic restraint. Half the novels I write are bombs whose manuscripts are currently moldering in a downtown storage locker. Things that do see the light of day I would describe as accidents forged by my demonic stick-to-it-iveness. *The Lucky Underdogs* was a haphazard stroke of good fortune. Some of my later published works were haphazard strokes of bad fortune. I am artistically related to the uninvited dinner guest who refuses to leave. You could compare me at work on a novel project to Ho Chi Minh at war in Vietnam for eighty years with the French, then the Japanese, then the French again, then the United States. If I finally publish the Magnum Opus I'll be like the North Vietnamese Army marching at last into Saigon on April 30, 1975, after six wars, three million deaths, and the complete defoliation of my country.

Sidebar: There is a criticism of Scott Fitzgerald's second novel quoted in Arthur Mizener's biography of Fitzgerald that I mentioned a few paragraphs ago. It says: "'*The Beautiful and Damned* is a real story, but a story greatly damaged by wit . . . the bane, not the making, of a true story-teller.'"

Q: If the shoe fits, should I wear it?

A: Who wants to know?

When I opened the door—surprise!—Ben's girl Jamie was standing on the stoop clutching in one hand a bouquet of flowers wrapped in pink tissue paper and in the other hand a cellophane-window takeout box with two multilayered napoleon cakelets from the Bob's Diner bakery inside it. Wow. Talk about reversals of fortune. I had never interacted with Jamie apart from Ben at her side.

"Hello, hello," I said, startled, flustered, suspicious, and immediately guilt-ridden. "Come in, come in."

"I'm not disturbing you? This will only take a minute. I hate to interrupt the artist at work. It's my lunch hour."

"No no, not at all, please please."

Stepping aside, I allowed her over the threshhold. To what nefarious motivation did I owe this visit? Jamie looked fabulous in an elegant linen blazer, a pastel orange blouse, a fashionably tight not quite knee-length skirt, and modestly high heels. Even a magnifying glass would have failed to locate an out-of-place curly hair on her shapely head. Given my propensity to shoot first and ask questions later I would have married her in a heartbeat after our first date. What's taking Ben so long to pop the question?

I experienced a surge of envy for my son as Jamie glanced around in panic at my disheveled kitchen, asking, "Do you have a vase-like thing I could put these flowers in? I'm so sorry about your broken arm. Ben told me the story. I also brought you your favorite pastry from Bob's Diner according to Ben. Not my idea but I'm suspending judgment this once. Don't forget to take your Lanoxin."

"Oh my goodness, *thank* you." I graciously accepted from her the flowers and the napoleons and then pivoted around, helplessly, wondering what sort of receptacle I could scrounge up for the flowers. "A vase-like thing?" She might just as well have asked me for a stuffed sea lion.

"Does it hurt? I mean your arm?" Jamie asked.

"Only when I laugh," I said, forgetting Jamie had a sense of humor devoid of a sense of humor.

"It was a terrible thing that happened," she said, gazing at me with what I took for genuine compassion. "It must have been awful to be attacked by a crazy man."

"Yes," I said, "it really broke me up." I can't help myself. It's a form of Tourette's. And it flew over Jamie's head like a goose migrating toward Corpus Christi at 30,000 feet in October.

"He could have killed you. It's so awful I can't stop thinking about it. Is there anything you need? Ben and I could bring things over after work. Chicken noodle soup? A bottle of Advil?"

"No no, I'm fine, thank you."

We stared expectantly at each other. *Here it comes,* I thought, *the fast break after the slow curve. She's going to inform me that Ben and Miranda have cancelled our hike and are committing me to the Living Center over behind Holy Cross Hospital.*

But all that happened is Jamie checked her slim little gold watch and said, "Uh-oh, I've got to run along, it's already almost two. I'll be crucified if I'm late." Then she said, "You're not really going to climb Spoon Mountain on your birthday, are you? Not with your arm like that?"

"I don't see why not," I said. "I don't walk on my arm."

That's when I realized Jamie must think I'm crazy. I mean, look at my crazy kitchen. Look at the crazy cast on my arm. Look at my crazy face that had not been shaved in four days. Look at the crazy clothes I was wearing, a filthy T-shirt, filthy khaki pants, and filthy cotton slippers from Bealls. Joe Slob. He can't stand putting on appearances even though his whole life is a lie. Explain *that.* And had Jamie known that earlier today I had abstained from pressing charges against Don the Man because of my inherent sympathy for the wretched of the earth she would have been vastly bemused by my inexplicably gonzo behavior. It's true: when they called me to come in and fill out the paperwork I demurred, saying "Let's not aggravate the situation." I could not even petition for a restraining order because that was the province of Magistrate Judge Rosalie Nesbitt, who, apparently, according to my girl Sally, was in a dalliance with my violent adversary whenever Father Rumaldo was preoccupied with his choirboys. (I should leave an anonymous tip on Randall Nesbitt's police-issue BlackBerry: "Hey, you ignorant dick, your wife is humping a bead squeezer *and* a born again.") "Maybe you could ask him to wear an ankle bracelet," I had suggested timidly. "Otherwise, leave me out of it. You catch more flies with honey than with vinegar."

"Say hello to Ben for me," I called after Jamie as she retreated toward her nifty late-model Mini Cooper. I still had a premonition we'd left something unsaid.

"No problemo," Jamie called back to me as she tootled once heading out of the driveway while I waved good-bye.

And then it hit me, too late, right between the eyes. Jamie, hard-hearted Jamie, had brought me the yummy napoleons. Jamie had brought me *flowers.*

Twenty

Yes, of *course* the Floresta shut down the national forest because of the fire danger, God damn their eyes. Six days shy of my birthday. I could not believe their audacity. I reread the announcement twice. All of the national forest or nearly all anyway. That meant half the county was now out-of-bounds and the fines for trespassing could be up to five thousand dollars. *Five thousand dollars?* Híjole! Even Tecolote Hill, my training path at the mouth of Sierra Canyon, was CLOSED DUE TO EXTREME FIRE DANGER. *Heresy.* In fact, the only "local" trail left open as a sop to tourists was the well-beaten and easily navigated track to Gallegos Lake in the wilderness area, but everywhere beyond the lake had been declared off-limits including Gavilán Peak and Spoon Mountain. After my first blush of outrage I decided: Screw you, Smokey. I don't care. *Hikers of the world, unite!* "Nobody but nobody stops me from my appointed rounds on my sixty-fifth birthday." If this was a foolish declaration, so what? Hadn't I spent a lifetime, against all odds, publishing books and writing screenplays despite debilitating illnesses and cockeyed relationships? Face it, I've always been a player. That meant that a few days from now Ben and Miranda and I were going to easily break

the law by climbing Spoon Mountain because the Forest
Service had only ten rangers to patrol five hundred thousand square miles, hence they could never in their wildest
dreams catch yours truly and my progeny who would be
transformed by then into your basic Marxist-Leninist ecoliberation invisible needles in a haystack: *We'll wear cam-
ouflage outfits and oakleaf tundra netting to outfox those
inept government flunkies patrolling the ridges with their
noisy helicopters—*

Later that day around dusk I was driving home after
warming up for Spoon Mountain by illegally climbing
Tecolote Hill once again. *Resist much, obey little.* Though
I had been nervous the entire time, nobody had cited me
for breaking the law. I was too sly, too clever, too surrepti-
tious, a fleeting shadow on the land, also a desperate man
who would kill you with a single karate chop if you were
meshuga enough to attempt an arrest before next Monday,
you dumb cluck. *I mean it.* Years ago I promised my children the moon and they are still waiting for it, so get out of
my way, Uncle Sammy, I don't drive with my horn.

A murky sky stretched away, smoke pollution almost
obliterating Boulder Peak down south, a full moon choking
on its own fading lustre through the noxious haze. *Roast
in hell, planet.* I cruised through town and parked behind
Bob's Diner. The spot was becoming my new home away
from home. Seven ravens were pecking at bags of wasted
edibles topping off the two commercial dumpsters by the
back door. The birds strutted about and leaped and fluttered, posturing at each other like insolent hip-hop rag-
pickers as they gorged on calories. From my open window

I gave a call, and, glancing my direction, a bird squawked in return. As I buffed up for Spoon Mountain conversing with ravens was becoming a whole new reenergized skill highlighting my linguistic devolution away from alphabetized language back toward the saner twittings of birds, bats, and bark beetles. You *can* go home again. *A wind is rising and the rivers flow.* Gooning at those gluttons pillaging stale donuts, French fries, pickles, and half-eaten hamburger patties while I spouted foolish gobbledegook at them in public was building up my psychic energy for the Spoon Mountain climb. Frankly, it's much easier to communicate with ravens if your own species has abandoned sanity in favor of the abyss.

Suddenly, all seven iridescent black scavengers acknowledged my presence by bristling their throat hackles and pantaloon feathers. One flared his "ears" at me. I got goosebumps and could almost envision them as royal birds of a natural realm perched on the carcass of an elk killed by wolves in Yellowstone. Almost. I wanted to reach out like Adam's hand on the Sistine Chapel ceiling and touch my fingertip to the beak of God. *Shazam.*

Then they returned to work and I drove off waving good-bye with a tear in my eye: "See you up on the mountain, boys and girls."

Twenty-one

"They closed the national forest," Miranda said over the telephone. "That's it. Our trip is postponed on account of global warming."

"No it isn't," I said. "That doesn't mean anything. Nobody will notice us. They have only six rangers to cover ten million square miles."

"Ben won't break the law, Dad, you know him. He has more rectitude than Billy Graham. He always puts a quarter in the parking meter. He never drives over the speed limit. He pays his bills on time. Ben can't steal a newspaper from the honor rack. He won't even eat a caramel from the supermarket candy bin to see if he likes it or not."

"If you tell him to hike, he'll hike."

"You don't know Ben," she said. "Ben hates publicity more than anything else. If we get arrested it'll be all over the newspapers because you're a public figure."

"I *used* to be a public figure, Miranda. Back in the Mesozoic Era when dinosaurs still roamed the best-seller lists. These days I'm more anonymous than anonymity itself."

She was right, though: Ben hates publicity. He is a really private person. He could never give a talk in public, for example. Ben never discloses who he voted for. For all

I know he might be a Republican. You can't pin him down politically because he listens a lot yet never commits himself out loud. Ben does some things that give him away, however. He volunteers twice a week at the wellness center to hand out information about diabetes and to comfort children (and their parents) who have recently been diagnosed with the disease. He's also on the board of a county raptor rescue team that drives wounded owls and hawks down to a wild animal vet in the Capital City. Ben participates in the Big Brother program because he likes kids. And he flies in the Skywatch plane during info-gathering trips over the forest.

No, he won't stand up in public and call attention to himself, though every now and then you might notice his shadow in the background.

Miranda is Ben's opposite. (Duh.) Miranda is outspoken. (Duh.) She is a fervid Democrat with socialist proclivities she inherited from me who has no problem shoving her opinions down your throat . . . in private. Or at least down *my* throat in private. However, she does not make a fool of herself in public. Unlike yours truly, she knows when to say when. She would never quork out loud at ravens in public behind a restaurant. In politics she works at the precinct level, attending all the caucuses, she is always a convention delegate, also a Hospital Workers' Union spokesperson. She is an organizer. When Miranda sees things wrong her instinct is to right the ship. Yet her aggressivity is not like mine—too loud, overemotional, embarrassing. She can deliver her opinions on an even keel. Miranda is good at addressing the unconvinced. She never bullies or talks down to people or ridicules with sarcasm. Her sarcasm is mostly reserved for me. With others she creates an even playing field and folks appreciate that. What they have never appreciated is my way of saying, "If you're pro-life you're an idiot," or, "The only good CEO is a dead CEO."

"That's a great way to turn off everybody," Miranda rebuked me at age fourteen. I told her to mind her own business. It took decades for me to realize she was correct. But now, at long last, I am in the process of reforming. Case in point: Back on page 19 I effectively vowed to stay off of a Stalinoid soapbox while writing this story. So far, when I have experienced the itch I have reminded myself to take another Valium and count to ten. Believe me, you don't want me to get started on the greenhouse effect or U.S. imperialism because I become like that derailed train in *The Fugitive*, the theater-release version starring Harrison Ford and Tommy Lee Jones. Unpleasant zealotry tends to inhabit my left-wing rhetoric like pod children from an alien planet's high school debating team.

Here's an example: A few days back I typed an enraged letter to the editor of our local newspaper. It was all about bears and what we do to them. This time, Magistrate Judge Rosalie Nesbitt's husband, Randall, the infamous deputy sheriff (and cuckold), had gotten a call from the manager at Super Save complaining that another destitute bear driven out of the shriveled mountains was in back of the store robbing a dumpster of spoiled cabbages. So Deputy Nesbitt showed up and blasted the animal once with buckshot from his sawed-off riot shotgun. The bear tumbled from the dumpster, and, confused, climbed up a nearby telephone pole and bumped into a transformer that shocked it with 20,000 volts of electricity. On fire, that bear fell to the pavement and burned to death, just one more ursine notch on Randall Nesbitt's gun.

At the end of my letter I called for all cops to be given the electric chair, the bastards. And then the town council should be impeached for approving a budget that included police protection from those antibear fanatics. Protection from *what*? And laws should be passed condemning any private citizen who harmed a bear to life imprisonment in solitary at the state pen. If Game and Fish ever terminated a so-called problem bear without extreme cause (say if the bear had devoured a child under two years of age), the wardens involved should be whiplashed, demoted to the lowest rung on the government ladder, and transferred to around-the-clock duty in Death Valley protecting the Devil's Hole pupfish population from predators (coyotes, Gila monsters, German tourists).

Obviously, I was making a point by being sarcastic. I did not feel sarcastic, however. I felt murderous. Night after night I lay in bed repeatedly watching that poor bear skydive to the pavement on fire. And I swore that the time has come to forsake reasoned discourse in our arguments for social justice and ecological preservation. You can't defeat the Philistines with "Please" and "Thank you." Polite words have never worked before. Better to line those bourgeois fat pigs and running dog lackeys of corporate warmongers up against the paredón and blow them to smithereens with AK-47s.

Calm down. Relax. I never sent the broadside. Some

newspaper readers might not have understood. They might have thought I was a wild-eyed madman screaming obscenities out through a metal grate in the grimy dungeon of a fourteenth-century loony bin. So that restraint is part of the New Me. I'm working to change my narrative and reconfigure my inner models, and I hope this will lead to personal limerence. I also pray it earns me brownie points, because I need them.

"We are not breaking the law to climb that mountain," Miranda told me over the phone.

"Oh yes we are," I replied. "We owe it to each other."

Twenty-two

My granddaughter Lizzy and I talk on the telephone. We are BFFs. (Look that up on your Twitter account.) Lizzy likes to chat with me long distance. She is a garrulous and bright child. One of our rituals is we converse in Raven with each other. I've decided to teach her the lingo. I sent her a CD of raven calls that I bought through Aaron Osborne's Internet connection and I ordered one for myself. Ravens communicate with each other using a wide array of croaks, mutters, knocks, trills, chortles, quorks, and gurgles. You can even mistake certain of their noises for xylophones. Last autumn, when Michael and Miranda last visited my town, I took Lizzy over to Bob's Diner so we could observe ravens feeding at the dumpsters behind the restaurant. I brought along binoculars for us to use. Lizzy was fascinated. We've been talking Raven with each other on the phone ever since.

Miranda can't stand it. "You're turning her into a linguistic freak, Dad. I don't want you pulling her down to your level. She goes to bed every night with that Raven CD playing on repeat. I have to sneak in and turn it off when she begins snoring."

Yeah, yeah. Tell it to the judge. On the phone Lizzy

will say, "Croak . . . croak," and I will reply with my xylophone imitation. The proper answer from Lizzy would be a throaty gurgle repeated at one-second intervals. Perhaps I'll counter with a flurry of guttural knocks. We can keep it up for at least five minutes until we collapse in laughter.

Periodically, Lizzy and Miranda and I confer together on their speakerphone. Lizzy keeps bugging Miranda and Michael for a cell phone of her own, but they would not kowtow to her wishes even if Vesuvius was erupting in their backyard.

Michael says, "Elizabeth, cell phones are costly and they're also a big distraction for a young person who's not old enough to understand how to control the technology, using it to her benefit without allowing it to become intrusive."

One of Michael's blind spots is he thinks you can reason with kids. For her part, Lizzy would like to enroll her folks in No Parent Left Behind. She would test them every three months and cancel their funding if they failed.

Miranda is more tuned-in than Michael. "Lizzy," she says, "you're barely old enough to drink coffee for breakfast, watch porn on the Internet, and have a martini before dinner. What makes you think you're ready for a cell phone?"

Lizzy is too smart to reply, "All my friends have cell phones." Basically, they don't. So instead she'll ask, "What happens if I get kidnapped from school by a pervert?" Or: "Suppose I have a life-threatening asthma attack while you and Dad are elsewhere?"

Michael will clear his throat. "Don't exaggerate, Elizabeth."

"You've never had an asthma attack in your life," Miranda will remind her.

"Well, suppose Poppy has a near-fatal asthma attack while we're taking a nature walk or watching a movie at the Ten Plex? He doesn't even have a cell phone. Our geese would be cooked."

"Goose," Michael corrects, as if English grammar relates to this discussion. When Michael sticks to plumbing he is fail-safe. In other fields he is way more iffy.

"Poppy always carries an inhaler," Miranda replies. "Now bag it, darling, you don't even remotely have a case."

"Well, how come I can't climb Spoon Mountain with you grown-ups?" Lizzy will posit. "You are so prejudiced against children."

Michael states the obvious: "Your legs are too short, Elizabeth, and your lungs aren't big enough yet. But don't despair, your time will come."

Lizzy is relentless, it's the family disease. "I never get tired in a jump rope contest. I can do tricks for an hour straight without stopping. I could climb Spoon Mountain backward doing Fast Jessicas all the way up." *Just ask her, she's a mensch.*

"Sure," Miranda says, "and next week Hannah Montana will release a death metal CD."

"I hate Hannah Montana," Lizzy proclaims. Her current favorite band is Paramore because they are in the *Twilight* movie, which I understand is all about tweenage vegetarian vampires. Maybe Lizzy and I will attend the movie together at the Ten Plex . . . if a cow falls down the badger hole and cars are made of green cheese. I am not a big fan of tween movies. In fact, I don't even attend regular movies anymore, I've had my fill unless they are documentaries by Michael Moore. Despite some of its adult content, Lizzy has seen *The Lucky Underdogs* twelve times. She thinks I'm God. And, by the way, could I please obtain for her an autograph from Melanie Griffith? As if Melanie Griffith and I were bosom buddies. I *wish*.

"Poppy," Lizzy asked me straight out during one of our non-speakerphone confabs, "why do you want to break the law by climbing Spoon Mountain with Mom and Uncle Ben on your birthday? Are you a criminal?"

"No, we're not really breaking the law," I said. "We used to climb in the mountains a lot and then we didn't climb up there anymore. So we need to go back before it's too late. God understands."

"We don't believe in God," Lizzy said.

"That doesn't mean She doesn't understand," I said.

"Are you guys really going to wear metal helmets with lightning rods poking up from the top of them on your heads during the hike?" Lizzy remarked.

"Are we *what*?"

"Mom says you're all going to wear metal helmets with twelve-foot-high lightning rods on top in order to make the excursion more interesting." Where does she learn to use words like "excursion" and "elsewhere"? (cf. above).

I said, "Yes, Lizzy, we are going to wear those helmets and also, when we reach the top of Spoon Mountain we plan to drink poison Kool-Aid and then fly off the mountaintop strapped to bright red hang gliders."

Lizzy said, "That's not funny. I don't want you to drink poison Kool-Aid and die."

"I'm not going to die," I said. "I was only joking."

Lizzy wasn't buying it. "No you're not, Poppy. I heard Mom talking to Michael when they thought I was out of earshot."

Lizzy calls her dad "Michael" because he always addresses her as "Elizabeth" instead of as "Lizzy" and she doesn't like "Elizabeth" because it's too grown-up and she is still a kid. Lizzy doesn't actually want to be a grown-up yet because it's more fun being a kid except when she wants to be treated with more respect like a grown-up, for example apropos Spoon Mountain. Michael thinks that calling her "Elizabeth" is more respectful, but he totally misunderstands the concept.

"What did your mom say to your dad?" I asked Lizzy.

"She said you have one leg in the grave."

"One *foot* in the grave," I corrected.

"What. Ever."

"You're mother doesn't know anything," I said. "I'm as healthy as a horse."

"What kind of a horse?"

"A Percheron."

"Like the ones in the Budweiser ads at Christmas?"

"Exactly," I said. "How did you ever guess?"

"You're lying through your teeth, Poppy. I can hear it in your voice. Just because I'm only seven and a half doesn't mean I'm stupid."

"I know you're not stupid. But I'm okay."

"Mom said you had a heart attack. I heard her."

"It wasn't a heart attack. It was indigestion and I was feeling anxious. But now I feel great."

"I feel anxious, too," Lizzy said.

"Why is that?"

"Because I'm too young for you to die. You're not old enough yet."

"I'm not going to die," I said. Jesus, get *off* it, Lizzy. You and your one-track mind.

"Yes you are. Everybody dies. Even birds die. And dogs. Everyone dies sooner or later."

"Well, obviously. But I'm not ready yet. I have to see you grow up first and become a famous biologist who saves the earth and stops Antarctica from melting."

"Don't try and change the subject, Poppy. I hate it when grown-ups pull the wood over my eyes."

"'Wool,' Lizzy, 'wool.' Like from a sheep. Not 'wood' from a tree."

"I said 'wool,'" Lizzy said, then she began to cry. I heard her snuffling and sucking in little gasps of air and making squeaky almost inaudible noises.

"What's happening?" I asked in alarm. "What are you doing? Are you crying, for Pete's sake? What is the *matter*?"

"Nothing is the *matter*," Lizzy sobbed, and she hung up on me.

Twenty-three

Naturally, after that happened the panic hit. When a child can see through you the jig is up. The plain fact is I don't want to lose my connection with Lizzy or with Ben or Miranda or anyone else. Yet I can feel a disaster approaching from right around the bend. It's on the wrong track and it's heading for me. Storm clouds are gathering, which should come as no surprise to anyone who has read this far. Late at night, every night, I get the jitters, the heebie-jeebies. I don't have to be a rocket scientist to know that my heart is in lousy shape and I should take better care of myself. I don't want me to die either. I should visit a cardiologist and submit to an EKG, an echocardiogram, even a catheterization, if necessary. No doubt I ought to be taking ACE inhibitors and beta-blockers along with my Coumadin and Digitalis. No more boozing and a changed diet would help. But I live in denial, I guess. I seem to have a death wish. Me and the human race. Please explain that to me, is it genetic? Why do smokers smoke? How come nobody listens to Lester Brown or Helen Caldicott? After I beat endocarditis and survived open-heart surgery eleven years ago I predicted I was in for a rough haul. Instead of playing it cautious, however, I embraced my own derailment with open arms even though I understood the consequences. I'm lucky to have survived this long. Now it's time to pay the piper. I don't slouch around muttering "I should have behaved differently," because I understand that what's done is done and regrets are dead-end nostrums on the road to nowhere. You live by the sword you die by the sword, so quit complaining.

Good advice, yet who wants to pay the piper? First the rats? Then the children? It's a lose-lose situation. I mean, lately I can't stop thinking about what I shared with Miranda and Ben before their childhoods were sabotaged by adolescence and we left nature behind. Though I didn't want to leave nature or my children behind I turned my back on both of them. But all I really yearn for now are those halcyon days again, especially for our sojourns at high altitudes before the drought began. I can't help myself. Rewind history, please. I want another chance. I would sell my soul to the devil for one more alpine excursion with my kids. Why do you think I've been so insistent?

The summer camping at Gallegos Lake and hikes up Spoon Mountain were unforgettable. Every day was special. Snug in sleeping bags we listened to owls and coyotes. Neither Ben nor Miranda was ever intimidated. We saw bighorn lambs cavorting across late-spring snowfields on the west side of Gavilán Peak. Golden eagles soared with the thermals. Gray jays landed on our fingertips to peck up raisins, arrogant as you please. Crossing boulder fields we listened to pikas chirping or to marmots giving their sharp whistles. In lush alpine marshes my kids pushed through arrowleaf groundsel, larkspur, and corn lilies up to their chins. We were in tune with the biology that sustains us.

On the summit of Spoon Mountain we photographed each other grinning as we made V signs. Sparrow hawks hovered stationary on the wind above the ridgeline. We sat on top of the world eating sandwiches while nearby ravens waddled about the tundra hunting grasshoppers. How not to be awed by the panorama?

Those few summers were our moment in Eden. We sheltered under Engelmann spruce branches during afternoon rain showers while hummingbirds buzzed at nearby flowers. We lay on our backs pressing against shooting stars and bluebells while admiring kettle flights of ravens that circled up into white clouds and blue sky. Seated on rock outcrops we peered through binoculars at massive scree slides, boulder fields, and avalanche chutes. One evening just at twilight we watched a cinnamon bear and her two cubs across a ravine feasting on the umbels of oshá plants. Ben finally learned to identify a Townsend's solitaire, an olive-sided flycatcher, and the blue grouse we flushed on Spoon Ridge that Miranda mistakenly thought were ptarmigans. She still claims they were ptarmigans even though she is wrong. I know blue grouse when I see them. I have bumped off dozens during the season in September, plucked them, wrapped bacon around their midriffs, subjected their plump little bodies to ninety minutes at 350 degrees Fahrenheit, then consumed their tender meat garnished by wild rice and mint jelly. You can't fool me about blue grouse.

We never tired during daylight hours; we slept under the stars at night.

On our last Christmas vacation together we made a half-dozen day-trips to Gallegos Lake wearing snowshoes. I wanted to see bighorn sheep during their rut. The winter was spellbinding. Spruce trees covered by glittering snow resembled Advent calendars and Hallmark cards. Twice we broke trail ourselves in two feet of new snow bundled up like Arctic explorers. Chickadees flitted through evergreen branches dislodging puffs of white. At Gallegos Lake we saw bighorn rams far above us butting heads while snow banners caused by gale-force winds whirled off the sawtooth rock piles.

We identified pine marten and weasel and red squirrel tracks on the forest snow. There was the odd-shaped route of a porcupine. We never tarried for long up there, it was too cold. An avalanche had erased a section of trail lower down snapping off hundreds of trees and coating thicker trunks with snow blast up to twenty feet. In the car we drank hot chocolate from a thermos and gobbled sandwiches, ravenous for the calories.

One night Miranda could not sleep. A thermometer by our kitchen door read ten below zero. "How do they survive up there?" she asked. "The sheep. How do the gray jays and chickadees stay alive? It must be thirty below zero in the mountains."

"Bighorns are animals from the Pleistocene," I explained. "They have different metabolisms than us."

"But how do they *stand* it?" she said. "They'll all be dead by morning. I don't want them to die."

She was crying. Miranda never cries. Miranda is the toughest kid I ever knew. I gave her a hot chocolate and sat beside her on the bed. I can't stand it when youngsters cry. "I'm going to freeze to death just thinking about them." She was serious and would not be assuaged.

Finally I said, "Mandy, I'll lie beside you and keep you warm. Nothing bad will happen."

"Yeah, right," she replied. "Life is a fairy tale."

Miranda did not push me away when I lay atop the covers beside her. After a while she fell asleep. I remember that occasion with a special pang because not often was I able to comfort my prickly daughter. Not often did the opportunity present itself. For an hour before I tiptoed away from her that night I too thought about the bighorn sheep bedded among rocks above 13,000 feet under a clear night sky at thirty below. And even as I wondered how *do* they survive such weather extremes I knew those animals are biologically programmed to be in that environment under those conditions. What I did not realize until years later is that Miranda also understood bighorns are ably suited for their tribulations and she was not worried about the sheep. She was crying for us. For Ben and herself and for me. She was crying for our camping trips in the mountains, and for all the trees and flowers and insects we had identified, for all those wild things she had scoffed at on the surface while treasuring them underneath. And she could not bear to think that our adventures with sickletop louseworts and hermit thrushes might be over soon. Already she was bereft. That kid was prescient. I should have paid way more attention.

Twenty-four

So why do all the grown-up women in my life sound the same? Maybe it's something I ate? I have listened to their identical harangues repeatedly and they are wearing thin. Who's afraid of Virginia Woolf? *I'm* afraid of Virginia Woolf.

"Bueno, let me get this straight, Juanito," Sally said. "Your arm is broken. You're heart goes in and out of atrial fibrillation on an hourly basis. Neither of your children wants to climb that mountain with you. And the national forest is closed due to fire danger. Nevertheless, you wish to break the law anyway despite the threat of a five-thousand-dollar fine and the risk to your health. Not to mention that you aren't turned on by me anymore."

"That was only once," I said, mortified. "I'm sorry. The McMansion intimidated me. It won't happen again."

"Whoa. Not so fast. I'm not blaming you for a brief spell of impotence. What sort of woman do you take me for? That isn't the issue at all."

She licked her lips, thinking for a moment. Then she said, "But here's the scoop, if you're interested, which I doubt. Bear with me and don't interrupt. Now that I'm almost fifty I admit I have become more goal oriented and I would like to be married again. Frankly, I'm tired of sneaking around and fending off middle-aged rakes. I hate 'dating.' I want Don off my back. I understand that you've been down that road before and so have I. We're both gun-shy. I also recognize that my three teenage boys are a handful that no sane bachelor would trade his freedom for. Makes sense, I can accept that too. I'm willing to sign a prenup that declares you can live in your house and I'll live in mine. All you need do is buy me a ring, make me an honest hooker. Otherwise, I have invested over a year in this relationship and it's beginning to dawn on me that you're growing skittish. And I wonder: Am I wasting my time by screwing just another fly-by-night remittance man who's now planning to ditch me because our sex has become routine and he is not intrigued by whatever else I have to offer? What do you think about that?"

Not *much*, for chrissakes.

We were seated at my kitchen table having a glass of wine. To be charitable, my kitchen is locked in a furor of squalid messiness, we already know that. To her credit, so far Sally has ignored the shambles. I understand her ulterior motives, women are transparent. Despite Alex, Zachary, and Jason, Sally's own digs are as clean and as spotless as the putting greens on the country club golf course she plays. I have stated earlier, however, that my girlfriend is drawn to the oddballs, the dissemblers, the dissolute. Therefore, during this past year she must have felt like a hungry goldfinch on a jumbo thistle-seed feeder with me. Then, unfortunately, Spoon Mountain became a fly in our ointment. Deliberately? Who knows. My motivations have always been murky. I flip-flop a lot.

When my third spouse and I briefly lived together in this house it was so swabbed and tidy you could lick maple syrup off the kitchen linoleum and actually *see* out windows that shone with a Windex clarity. Yes, my third wife was a "bipolar thespian." You may have caught her in some B horror movies in which she plays scantily clad nymphs who get raped and strangled or stabbed to death. There's a list of these pictures under her name in the cast index of the VideoHound's Golden Movie Retriever. She's a looker. Stage name of Laurinda Mallory. Surprisingly, she turned out to be a homebody eager to cook cornbread and cheese soufflés and sew curtains for the house when she wasn't riding her broom off to the Wicca orgies. We met on a set and instantly "fell in love," or at least we "fell in sex" and had an intense marriage that lasted two years, during which, to refresh your memory, I caught endocarditis, went into congestive heart failure, had open-heart surgery, and almost died. We both awoke at the bottom of a cliff wondering "What happened?" Our relationship had been like two people trapped inside a gigantic washing machine locked in the spin cycle. As luck would have it, Laurinda had money from her "acting" and in the divorce settlement asked only for our wedding china and to be free of my hex on her. Father Rumaldo performed the exorcism in court before Magistrate Judge Rosalie Nesbitt who was young then, only in her first term. It's a small southwestern mountain town, get used to it.

Today, my kitchen counters and the table are piled high with manila envelopes, manuscripts, old letters and books, empty cereal boxes, broken staplers, a cheap CD player from RadioShack, an accordion file of tax receipts, and so forth and so on. Cookie's rancid pillow on the table is so covered with accumulated cat hairs it could pass for a little dead yak. Chez moi, the glut never sleeps. There's no space in my kitchen for things that belong there, say a toaster, a microwave, or a dish rack. Only two stove burners function and I have not lit the oven for eight years because it might explode.

It requires scant insight to realize that herein dwells a man whose most recent novel was published seven years ago and sank like a stone. It was called *Bury My Heart at Peyton Place*. Seriously. Case closed.

"I don't see myself as just another fly-by-night remittance man," I said. Sally was looking at me over the rim of a wineglass raised almost to her lips. She wore silver hoop earrings and an enigmatic smile. I confess that she could have passed for an alluring not quite middle-aged Scarlett Johansson. And even though I was apprehensive about our forthcoming conversation I also felt like a fly-by-night remittance man who was eager to screw her. What a difference a day makes. When a beautiful woman is edgy the arousal factor rises exponentially. Talking about marriage is dangerous and dangerous is sexy.

"I love you," I added for good measure.

"Sure," Sally said by rote. "If I buy a ticket and get in line. At least Don the Man meant it when he spoke those words."

"Don the Man is a paranoid psychopath."

"Is that why you decided not to press charges?"

"If I had pressed charges how much time would he

do—a year, eighteen months?—and then what would happen to me when he got sprung? I'm offering an olive branch now while I have the chance."

On a bit of formerly open wall space in the kitchen I have a cork bulletin board on which are pinned family photographs and other tchotchkes which include three Zapatista dolls sent to me by fans and a Barry Bonds bobblehead figurine hanging off Mardi Gras beads. The pictures are of Ben and Miranda as kids (in baseball and basketball togs, and with their mother holding up a trophy) and of Michael and Miranda and Lizzy together (with a rat peeking from Lizzy's pocket and smirky Michael proffering a toilet plunger). There's also one of Ben and Jamie posing on cross-country skis. Rounding out the display are three portraits of Lizzy at different ages seated on the laps of red-nosed Walmart Santa Clauses sticking her tongue out at the camera.

Sally took a sip of wine and gestured her chin at the bulletin board. "Well, if you love me so much why isn't my picture on your wall? Where are all the snapshots you have of me? I know you've got one of me in my bikini beside the club swimming pool. And of me naked on your bed. And hitting a golf ball off the first tee in the Pro-Am last September. You also have a candid image of us together at the Kiwanis banquet you gave that ridiculous speech at. However, there's no evidence of me at all in this house. I might as well be invisible. Maybe if I was a mountain or a fish you'd tack a picture of me on your bulletin board. Or if I was a bighorn sheep?"

"Those are random family pictures," I said. "They are old

photos. I stuck them up a couple of years ago simply to fill a void. You have not been deliberately omitted, rest assured."

"'Rest assured?' Who's that woman with your kids?" Sally asked. "Apparently I have never paid attention."

"It's their mother, I guess." I squirmed. If Sally had never before paid attention to my kitchen bulletin board I'll be a monkey's uncle. *Every* woman is Sherlock Holmes. They miss *nothing*.

"You 'guess'?" she said. "You guys had children together. What was she like? Why did you marry? What happened to end it? You never talk about her. Why is she in your rogues' gallery? Are you two still in love?"

"God no," I said to answer her last question. "Things simply went wrong" covered everything else.

"Okay, I've made a decision," Sally said. "I want my picture on display there with all the others. Go fetch one and pin it up. Right now. Prove that you 'love me with all your heart' even if you don't. It's a small gesture that might diminish my growing insecurity and paranoia." She jiggle-flicked her fingers at me. "Apúrate."

In the northeast corner of my bedroom were two Smith's shopping bags full of photographs. A file cabinet (I'm not sure which) contained a folder with the nude images of Sally (and of five former heartthrobs). Part of my bottom bureau drawer had packets of developed film with negatives. I'm so last century I have yet to go digital. Fortunately, one of the Smith's bags coughed up two pictures of Sally: bikini'd beside the club swimming pool, and holding my black cat Carlos in her arms. Carlos won't let himself be held by anyone except Sally, who knows why?

After pinning the photos to my bulletin board I stepped back, saying, "How's that? And for an encore would you like to make love with me?" By now I was seriously in the mood and had furtively popped a tab of instant virility while searching for the snapshots of Sally. Anyone who can afford the price of a prescription can diminish his girl's insecurity and paranoia, right?

Wrong.

"Not today, sweetie." That caught me by surprise. Sally rose, draining her glass of wine and rinsing it in the sink. "For some reason I'm still feeling petulant." She pinched and wiggled each side of her blouse, adjusting the bra underneath. "Perhaps I'm not in estrus right now. Yesterday I triple-bogied the fifth hole at the course and it's only a par 3. The idiot greens are turning brown from heat. Then Father Rumaldo tried to hit on me at the Nineteenth Hole where he was having drinks with my enemy, Max González, who's selling the church the Alfred Myers property next door to the Saint Vincent de Paul House. I had a piece of that listing until Max gave Alfred a kickback for letting him have an exclusive on the place. So I'm a smidgen tired of being jerked around by men, you included. In fact, I think I've changed my mind, I don't even want my pictures on your bulletin board. Isn't that just like a woman? Remove them, please. I had to twist your arm to get them tacked up there in the first place, but apparently you only went to the trouble because you want to get laid. And I think that's a poquito superficial, don't you?"

Sometimes you can only gape mutely in astonishment at the person facing you.

"Furthermore," Sally said, "you claim you'd like to bond with your children on top of Spoon Mountain? That's a nice sentiment and I commend you for it, although I'm wondering when are we—you and me—allowed to bond on a special occasion? Maybe for once in your life will you even say 'I love you' to me and mean it? Anymore, you seem to be acting as if emotional proximity is equal to Anthrax bacteria and I don't like that very much."

Lifting her purse off my kitchen table, she reached inside it to retrieve a compact and a tube of lipstick.

"To be truthful," Sally said, "I've got a lot of other things to do besides begging you to marry me. For example: In a minute I have to hit the First State drive-up window because I need cash to pay off Jason's faux pas with Magistrate Judge Rosalie Nesbitt's grandmother in the Furr's parking lot two weeks ago. Rosalie will take the money under the table and erase the ticket and play the lottery with my fine. I feel like squealing to her about Father Rumaldo's sexual harassment. Of course, I should squeal to Rosalie's husband, the trigger-happy deputy sheriff, about *her* misbehavior with Father Rumaldo, a *priest* no less. God is turning over in His grave."

She clicked open the compact, holding the mirror in front of her face, and carefully applied the lipstick.

"Sadly, I'm afraid to tattle on anybody," Sally continued, "because the grandmother is so unbalanced she'll put a curse on Jason who already gave her his life savings to pay for her car, which is going to have the bodywork done by none other than your biggest fan, Don the Man, whom they have released from his cage not even wearing an ankle bracelet, those stupid rednecks, because you were too munificent to press charges. I hate to say this but you must be seriously impaired, honeybunch. Your pinko chivalry is out of control."

Sally dropped the lipstick tube and the compact back into her purse and plucked a Kleenex from a box on my table, folded it in half and slipped it between her lips and pressed her lips closed a couple of times to dab off excess gloss.

"And have I mentioned that Don the Man and Judge Rosalie are cozying up to each other despite her trysts with Father Rumaldo? I hate this town. I really should phone Randall Nesbitt an anonymous tip. Maybe *I* don't want *Don* to be a bad example for our kids? Then I must show a client from Chicago the Abel Martínez hacienda in Los Córdovas where we'll be lucky if the renter doesn't sic his pit bull on us, the guy is loco in the coco. Too bad, I'm a working girl and if I don't put food on the table my three sons will rob a 7-Eleven or start a meth lab to earn spending cash . . . over my dead body."

Sally clicked shut her purse, opened a cabinet door under my sink, and dropped her tissue into the wastebasket.

Was she finished? Not yet. "And now hear this," Sally said. "While we're on the subject. This morning I met your son's girlfriend Jamie at the title company because I needed to finish up some legwork for a closing next week si dios quiere (which I seriously doubt). But anyway. Right in the middle of our confab Jamie had a tearful nervous breakdown and begged me to ask you to order your son Ben to finally marry her because she wants to have a kid before hitting menopause. I said, 'Jamie, we're at work here, I'm not a psychiatrist or a fertility doctor, I'm a real estate bro-ker. Plus asking Ben's dad to promote marriage is like ask-ing a sumo wrestler to plug Slim-Fast.' So she dried her eyes and we finished the deal. I must admit, however, that girl put a flea in my ear.'"

I lifted a finger: "Point of order—"

"And meanwhile," Sally continued, "in defiance of all logic you're planning to climb that mountain with your kids? You don't listen to me, you listen to nobody. If God spoke to you from a burning bush you'd reach for a fire extinguisher. You think your children will suddenly love you if you threaten to kill yourself by climbing a mountain with them? What would happen if you took them to a piz-zeria, ate a hearty meal together and drank a few beers, had a mature conversation, and hugged each other afterward? Is that too straightforward for you? Is it too *easy*?"

My girlfriend walked over to the kitchen door and opened it.

"So there you have it," she said. "I sound like a jilted novia in a telenovela, don't I? The camera should now zoom in for a close-up of my lower lip quivering, my boobs fall-ing out of my bandeau top, and salty mascara dripping off my chin. I sound whiney, don't I?, and God hates a whiner. So that's enough whining for the moment, I reckon. Hasta luego, borrego."

Gone.

What?

Just like that.

I scurried after Sally, catching up as she approached her car across my driveway.

"Wait. Please stay," I blurted. "I admit it, I'm a jerk, will you marry me?"

Sally turned and her expression jolted me. She has beautiful green eyes, I've described them before. In them there is always warmth even if she's miffed, a playful and insouciant gleam. No matter what, the connection is also seductive and loving, she can't help it. Imagine my surprise, then, to note that all light had drained from her beautiful green eyes and they were dead. No love, no humor, no puzzlement, no nothing, just dead. Flat affect. That stopped me cold.

"'Marry me?'" she said. "Are you kidding? Gee, my prayers are finally answered. You really want to get laid that badly? Well, go fuck yourself, you coward. Then drop dead twice."

And she got in her car and drove away.

Twenty-five

That hurt.

It's late and I'm sitting at the word processor pouring out my heart in a fifteen-page letter to Sally imploring her not to leave me, I'll change my wicked ways, I really truly love her, she's the best thing that ever happened to me, I'm sorry, I'm so sorry that I've acted like such a coward . . . when those scaredy-cats Cookie and Carlos banged through the cat door and skidded past me headed for the bedroom closet and at the same moment I heard a terrible crashing sound outside the kitchen door. *Oh wonderful.* Had Don the Man arrived to mete out added punishment because I had refused to press charges, making him a free man with nothing to do except promulgate more murder and mayhem? I should have flung the book at him. Of course anyone could be out there because all kinds of lunatics dropped by my place at ungodly hours. A total stranger had appeared shortly after eleven p.m. one night, beeped his horn, and demanded that I contribute two hundred dollars to the Mumia Abu-Jamal defense fund in Philadelphia. Another screwball entered the driveway and fired a pistol toward the sky screaming *"Up yours you friggin' eco-freak!"* A young woman showed up at four a.m. covered with dust, all messed up on crack and ecstasy, her lower lip bleeding as she beseeched me for shelter because some wasted tecatos were chasing her. When I drove her home to a rattletrap trailer behind the armory she attempted to borrow twenty bucks, then produced a joint from her pocket and wanted to turn on together, cursing me when I declined: "I hated *The Lucky Underdogs!*" They materialized from the violent night and disappeared back into it. I keep a loaded .22 pistol in my top bureau drawer underneath the socks but I fear that gun, I have never removed it from the dresser. How can one human being point a weapon at another human being? What do you do, yell "Suck on this, you infidel!" and then pull the trigger? Yet I inhabit a violent town, I was once a controversial public figure, and it is no secret where I live.

Plus I imagine everybody wants to squash my Spoon Mountain expedition now that the national forest has been closed due to fire danger. Who knows, maybe even Ben and Jamie, those borderline quislings, were outside determined to scare me straight. Despite the Bob's Diner napoleons and the flowers I don't trust Jamie farther than I can toss Ben's Toyota. The leopard never changes its spots. And I wouldn't have put it past Miranda and Michael to have driven north for the party, although sensible Michael has usually steered clear of our family squabbles—

Suddenly I snapped and leaped to the top bureau drawer for my .22 pistol. No more Mr. Nice Guy. It was time to fight fire with fire, I'm a U.S. American, aren't I? Buck up, you sniveling tub of guts. *Go ahead, make my day.* Then, armed and dangerous (though with my heart pounding), I sneaked across the kitchen to the door and listened. Some kind of type A aggressive mammal high on caffeine or peyote buttons picked up my plastic garbage dumpster on wheels and again hurled it against the outside wall.

I crouched to one side in case bullets came through the door as I called, "Hey, pal, what are you doing? Are you a brain-dead animal? I'm trying to bag a little shut-eye here. *It's three o'clock in the morning!*"

The assailant kicked the dumpster sideways, pummeled it with a big stick or a sledgehammer, and then punched apart sacks of garbage sounding like an elephant dancing flamenco atop sheets of gigantic bubble wrap.

"Yo, listen up!" I shouted. "I've got a gun in my fist and it's loaded! This isn't funny! Go home! Quit drinking. Who are you?"

For an answer the dumpster was vigorously punted against the wall once again, obviously the work of more than one person, say those three juvenile delinquents from Sally's family—Jason, Zachary, and Alex—bribed by their vindictive mom to create a vengeful uproar robbing me of sleep, rattling my nerves, and sabotaging my alpine hiking confidence. At this thought I grew way more irate than I was afraid—*basta ya!*—so I grabbed a flashlight from a basket on the sideboard and rashly unlocked the door.

"I have a gun you bastards and I'm coming out!"

I clicked on my flashlight, cocked the double action six-shot Harrington & Richardson model 649 revolver held in my left hand, and jerked open the door fully prepared to execute the interlopers or die trying. Keep in mind that I'm not Dirty Harry or even Rooster Cogburn, I'm an almost sixty-five-year-old man with a bad heart condition, asthma, a potbelly, and zero equilibrium. Just for starters. I won't even mention my personal life.

Twenty-six

A single bear froze, caught by the flashlight's beam. A male bear. I'm not sure how I knew that, but I knew. Or sort of a male bear, anyway, missing half one ear with much of his fur matted or crusted by blood or snot or by rotting gobs of free-range organic buffalo meat stew rich in antioxidants, and he probably weighed less than a hundred and thirty pounds. He was seated eight feet away beside the overturned dumpster surrounded by a pile of shredded paper and plastic yogurt containers and other rubbish, a week's accumulation because collection day was tomorrow. Over my entire life I had seen only a trio of wild bears, all three spotted from a distance while I was grouse hunting with Roberto Salazar, and they had been departing vertiginously in the opposite direction. This bear was not running in any direction, however. He blinked his beady eyes, or at least one beady eye, the other had been mashed back into the socket. Over the long pointy snout was draped an empty plastic sack that had held frozen peas I had consumed for dinner three nights ago. The bear's posture, with front paws clutched against a furry chest that had a white patch rising biblike to a ring around the neck, made him appear a tattered yet somehow cuddly teddy bear.

I waved my cheap pistol at the animal saying, "Shoo, scat." The disoriented bear blinked again, then lifted one paw and plucked the bag off his nose revealing a scar across the bridge so distinct it could have been made by a hatchet. The gesture also called attention to his claws which were really large and very sharp. Did he have only two toes on one deformed foot? No. Sorry. To be polite I lowered my flashlight beam from the peculiar undersized eye and spoke again:

"Shoo. Scat. Go away from here."

Articles I have read about black bears insist that on ninety-nine percent of encounters they run away from people. Yet this bear had no intention of taking a powder. He continued to sit there made punchy by hunger no doubt, his one orb peeping at me while awaiting my next move.

And as the seconds blipped along I not only lost my fear but an unexpected calm smoothed my goosebumps and my aggravated heart quieted a bit. There are moments, even confronted by a blasted wreck like this, when awe is the only proper feedback. When was the last occasion I had been face-to-face with a wild thing commensurate to my capacity for wonder? Maybe the poor animal was an emissary from Spoon Mountain urging me not to give up the dream.

I closed my eyes and pinched my nose taking a deep breath, and when I opened up I said, "Get out of here. They really will waste you if you stick around any longer."

No deal. I'm not leaving. And in this drought where can I go anyway?

Okay, I aimed my pistol at the sky and fired a cheerful,

nonthreatening, good-bye-my-friend warning shot, an act that elicited immediate response. Lickety-split Scarface dropped to all fours, pivoted, and bolted smack against the side of the empty dumpster—*blonk!*—and with a strangled huff of panic then backed away among the scattered refuse heaps, whirled, and, obviously bewildered, charged directly at me, dumping me flat on my butt and catching his teeth against my left pant leg as I rolled off the stoop toward a patch of weeds. The pant leg ripped open right up the seam to my belt as I screamed and banged the bear on his head with my cast. Apparently that hurt, because Scarface hesitated, stunned, blinking that one little eye, then suddenly yelped, sprinted away, and disappeared.

Holy Methuselah.

Twenty-seven

It's my habit to stop by the Read & Feed Pre-Owned Book Emporium to shoot the breeze with Aaron and with Shirley, if she's around, although Shirley can put a damper on the palaver because she suffers from selective echolalia. But she was not there today. Roberto Salazar was, however, because he and Aaron have formed a relationship akin to the Odd Couple. Ever since losing his leg Roberto has become a serious reader. He spends hours perusing the shelves while gabbing with Aaron about Hemingway and Philip Roth, Zora Neale Hurston and Octavio Paz. Aaron is tepid on Paz but will advise patrons the Nobel winner is a god. He idolizes Hemingway and Philip Roth, though you'd never know it. In Aaron's eyes they can sell themselves, so why glorify? Should you contemplate purchasing a copy of *Love in the Time of Cholera* by Gabriel García Márquez, a "mega-genius" according to Aaron (in private), he will tell you beforehand that García Márquez "is so rococo *and* torporific you'll need an insulin shot every twenty pages." Don't ask me how, but that sells. Aaron's comment to me about a copy of *Moments of Reprieve* by Primo Levi that I once thought to acquire was, "It's just another Holocaust book with a heart of gold." Bingo! I reached for my wallet.

If Shirley is around she will say, "Oh, Aaron, you're such a contrarian." Then she will apologize to any customer present: "Ignore him, he's a little off his feed today."

That is a figure of speech. Aaron never quits gnawing on chocolate frosted donuts acquired daily from the pastry shop at Bob's Diner where my raven friends chow down at the trash receptacles in back. Aaron and I share a sweet tooth problem. His stomach is bottomless. He's always hungry. He is a legendary trencherman. Therefore, of course, Shirley is a vegan and weighs only about seventy pounds.

My bookseller friend is a giant who wears a fez on his large head and a Mexican serape over his bulging torso. Why the serape? You tell me. It and the fez are his signature pieces of attire. He could be a corpulent used-car salesman from Abù Dhabi or a formidable Las Vegas bouncer. For sure, he commands attention. When some people first enter the store they instinctively wince.

The cat, John Wayne Dahmer, always sleeps by the cash register and never wakes up. Shoppers pat him, scratch his ears, pull his tail, reach under and tickle his tummy, no reaction. He is a narcoleptic sphinx.

By contrast, Roberto Salazar is a good-looking guy, mid-fifties, who used to sell insurance, manage an office supply store, and run a sporting goods operation that featured customized bowling trophies (we have an eight-team league in town). He has dabbled in other businesses that also flamed out spectacularly. When it comes to entrepreneurial ventures Roberto has the Joe Btfsplk touch. Mr. Jinx. He is an eternal optimist, though, a divorcé and father of two like myself, and a former outdoors man whose style has been seriously crimped since his leg went south. He still fishes from a canvas deck chair on the Río Grande shore for catfish, bass, and pike. And he snags Kokanee salmon from a boat over at El Vado Reservoir in season. He has even sat in my car with me a couple of times spying on the Bob's Diner ravens through binoculars. We sipped Black Jack and reminisced about old times. Roberto thinks ravens are scalawag charros turned into birds by brujas. You have to take him with a grain of salt. But he cannot tramp around grouse hunting or stalking elk anymore and I miss our times together in the forest. We once had a lot of fun.

Toward the back of the Read & Feed are three old wicker armchairs browsers can utilize while sampling the merchandise. The nearby coffee machine dispenses a piping hot brew made from freshly ground beans sent directly from peasant co-ops in El Salvador. You can also purchase quaint little sandwiches composed of cucumbers, spinach leaves, and tofu cheeses on Ezekiel bread, a specialty of the house prepared by Shirley. The sandwiches, kept moist in Ziploc baggies, are displayed on a table beside a tray of éclairs, cream puffs, jelly donuts, and other savory toxins from Bob's. For years Shirley has fought those pastries, but you can't argue with Aaron or with his tastes. Plus, his toxins fly off the table in droves; the sandwiches are a complete bust, they never move.

So Roberto Salazar was camped on one of those wicker chairs, Aaron occupied another, and I held down the final seat. Music on the CD player was 1950s jazz, which Aaron really enjoys: Dave Brubeck, MJQ, Miles Davis, et al. I'm more of an Elvis fan. And I *love* Little Richard. Roberto prefers Selena, Country Roland, and Creedence Clearwater Revival.

"A bear?" Aaron said. "You've got to be kidding me. How stupid does a person have to be to open the door?" He had fetched me a washcloth wrapped around some crushed ice to press against my left eye swollen shut. There's a mini fridge in his office.

"I don't want to talk about the bear," I said. "I'm having a bad hair day."

"He didn't know it was a bear," Roberto said in my defense. "He thought it was a crazy intruder."

"Then that makes *more* sense to open the door?"

"I'd just as soon not talk about the bear," I reiterated. "Let's change the subject."

Roberto said, "Well, what would *you* do, Aaron, if you heard somebody smashing all your sale books in the carts on the sidewalk in front of the store?"

"I'd look out the plateglass window and see who or what was doing the damage before I opened the door. Actually, I would not open the door. I'd call the cops. Let them handle it."

"Suppose for the sake of argument there wasn't a plateglass window?" Roberto asked.

"There *is* a plateglass window," Aaron replied. "So that's not the issue."

In fact, not only is there a plateglass window, but in it Aaron maintains a pyramid of dust-covered trade paperback *The Lucky Underdogs*, which used to sell like hotcakes, though not anymore. I wish somebody, *anybody*, would purchase *one* of those books. At first the pyramid flattered me. Now it's a rotting albatross around my neck, a monument to my professional inconsequentiality. I'm afraid to say anything, though, for fear of seeming ungrateful. Once the DVD came out the novel walked a plank. Nobody *reads* me anymore. They simply watch the "charming" movie.

"Why don't we drop the topic?" I said. "Let's stop beating a dead dog."

Roberto said to Aaron, "Okay. What did you do when Don the Man came in here swinging a baseball bat a few days ago—stand behind the cash register and twiddle your thumbs?"

Aaron misunderstood the question. "There's nothing I could have done," he said. "What am I supposed to do, hire a pair of armed guards to flank the doorway whenever I sponsor a poetry slam or an open mike night?"

"Actually, Don's not a bad fellow," Roberto said, reaching for another donut. He rarely pays and Aaron lets him get away with it even though Shirley, who does the accounts, raises a ruckus. "Don and I once worked together," Roberto admitted. "I bought three used Bobcats at a state auction and he fixed them up for me. He's a great mechanic, a magician with his hands."

"A pox on his hands," I muttered under my breath.

"What happened to the Bobcats?" Aaron asked.

"I sold them to the Ace Garden Rental Center which promptly went Chapter 11 before I could deliver. Then Don maneuvered to broker a deal with the forest service that died due to government cuts when the economy nosedived. But Don tried hard for me. He's a stand-up guy."

"No he isn't," I mumbled sotto voce. Roberto was

beginning to seriously vex me with his Don-the-Man superlatives.

Aaron said, "That maniac invaded my store. He wreaked havoc. I hope they throw the book at him. If I thought he had a penny I'd drop this conversation and call a lawyer. And you, Mr. Revolutionary Big Shot," he accused, wagging a fat finger at me, "you refused to press charges? What are you, afraid he'll come after you when they let him out of jail? What if he attacks you again tomorrow because he is *not* incarcerated?"

"Aw, ease up, pal," Roberto said. "Believe it or not, Don is okay. I know he has a short fuse because of his ADHD issues. On occasion he forgets to take his medicine. Is that a felony? Who among us can throw stones? As for his jealousy issues regarding his ex-wife, they are not totally without foundation. Remember, it takes two to tango. With apologies to you, my friend, but honestly."

"'Honestly?'" I displayed my crippled arm in front of his face. If it had had a hook on the end I might have snagged it through one of his nostrils. "Look at what that bastard did to me."

"I know, I know." Daintily, Roberto pushed my fiber-glassed limb aside. "You have a legitimate complaint. From Don's point of view, however, he only wanted to get your attention. Obviously, he overreacted. He's very confused about the mother of his three boys, can you blame him? Didn't she dump you like a hot potato two days ago without even firing a shot first across your bow?"

"What does *that* mean?" I asked.

"It means she's an uppity chavala with more attitude

than Pancho Villa." Roberto poured himself another coffee with a splash of half-and-half and stirred it with a Read & Feed laminated bookmark. "She's too smart for her own britches," he continued. "I had an affair with her three years ago that lasted for two months, pardon my revelation. You're my friend, no offense, I'm not dissing you, and anyway she's not your girlfriend anymore and she wasn't your girl back then, either. She wouldn't let me pay for anything, not even a mojito at El Patio. 'I have money,' I said, 'I'm not a bum.' 'Stick your money where it won't get any sun,' she said, 'I don't want to be beholden.' Beholden? What is that? I threw up my hands. 'Let down your guard for a minute, woman, and let's have some more fun.' That's what I told her. As you must know she's great in bed. I hope that's not TMI. So you know what she told me back? She said, 'Take your plastic leg and make tracks, Jack.' That woman is an emotional basket case who—"

I hit him. I sprang clear of my chair and popped Roberto in the snoot, dislocating the pinkie of my left hand. Roberto went head over heels with such a thump his prosthetic leg came unbuckled, flying up out of his chinos and clonking me on *my* nose, breaking it as I barged into the same portable bookrack Don the Man had tipped over only days earlier. I landed among a cascade of pricey secondhand volumes that bounced off my noggin tearing their pages front, left, and center. Aaron fluttered his humongous hands attempting to catch some of those tomes before their spines broke from clobbering me. Basically, his efforts failed and I was buried under the books. Laugh and the world laughs with you, buddy; weep and you weep alone.

Twenty-eight

Miranda said, "Sorry, Johnny, you are *not* climbing Spoon Mountain tomorrow."

I replied, "Yes we are and nobody can stop us. I promised you and Ben, remember?"

Ben and Jamie were attending my birthday eve bash along with Michael, Miranda, and Lizzy, who were bunking at the Sagebrush Inn. Michael could have squashed me with one finger: How do the young grow so large and handsome and strong? He was wearing a Bart Simpson T-shirt and a People's Plumbing baseball cap. Michael has a wee diamond earring in his left earlobe and a tattoo of Mighty Mouse on his left bicep. It dates from long before he married Miranda. "I was a wanton youth," he is apt to chuckle.

The shiny sprite Lizzy was as cute as molasses wearing Mary Janes, a denim halter top, and a Pittsburgh Steelers baseball cap. That's who Michael and Miranda root for, the Pittsburgh Steelers. They are fanatics. They subscribe to the NFL channel so as not to miss a game. By default Lizzy must root for the Steelers also, otherwise her parents will disown her. "We'll put her out on the street wearing a placard around her neck that says WILL WORK FOR FOOD,"

Miranda has threatened more than once. Nobody trash-talks Big Ben and the boys in their bailiwick.

We were all crowded around the kitchen table of my prosaic hovel scarfing a repast that Ben and Jamie had contrived featuring a pot of linguini with mussels and scallops, steamed broccoli, and a salad of arugula, marinated artichoke hearts, and mung bean sprouts accompanied by several bottles of Perrier (because Ben and Jamie and Lizzy don't drink) and two bottles of Pinot Noir (because Miranda and Michael will have only one glass apiece yet I myself intend to become semi-snockered). Ben's dog Cujo was snoozing under the table with his lone ear cocked and an eye open waiting for Cookie or Carlos to blunder into the kitchen from their hiding place in my bedroom closet. You bet the cats hate visitors.

To accommodate everyone I had cleaned up the joint. Obviously, I needed to work hard on damage control before things got more out of hand.

"No we are not climbing with you tomorrow," Miranda said. "Look at yourself, have you checked a mirror lately? You could be a prisoner who was tortured at Abu Ghraib. Are you blind in that eye? Your nose is bigger than Cyrano de Bergerac's. Do you have any idea how ghoulish your face is? And now you not only have a cast on your right arm but also a splint on your left pinkie? Do you know what happens if you perform extreme exercise at high altitudes with all those contusions and broken blood vessels?"

"Doesn't matter," I said. "We are going."

Patiently, she said, "When you are better, maybe. After they reopen the forest. Why not? But now let's be rational.

Twice a week on the pediatric ICU I watch children succumb from you wouldn't believe what traumas. Car accidents, domestic cleansers, drug ODs, congenital heart defects. Under the right circumstances it's really easy for people to die. However, if you want to climb that mountain, fine. Only first get back into shape for two months, follow a diet, lose twenty pounds, and then we'll talk turkey after you do a treadmill that says you're game to go, fair enough?"

More than fair. It made perfect sense to me. A prudent strategy at last, thank God.

I said, "No, we have to do it right away on my birthday. If we don't do it immediately it'll never be done. Twenty years have already passed. I'm tackling that mountain tomorrow with you guys."

"No you aren't," Ben said. "And if you insist on going alone we'll notify the forest service that you're breaking the law and they'll post guards on the wilderness boundary at Gallegos Lake all day."

This was a major speech for Ben and he was almost breathless afterward. Me too. Ben is not a person who makes threats or snitches on people. At least not lightly. He appeared startled by his own inappropriate vehemence.

Miranda said, "We're not attacking you, Dad, you're attacking us. Suicide is a very aggressive act against the folks who love you the most."

I said, "Suicide, schmuicide. This is important. If it's postponed it will never happen. It has been postponed long enough."

"That isn't true," Ben said. "Pop, we're not disrespecting

you. We care about you and were ready to hike with you until they closed the forest and then this happened."

I jutted forward my split lower lip. "Balls, Ben. Tomorrow I climb that mountain. And you two will come with me."

Miranda said, "My dear old man, let me explain. Recently you nearly had a heart attack and wound up in the emergency room, and that mountain is almost thirteen thousand feet high. Ben and I will accompany you when you're healed but not until. And that's final. Since the heart scare three weeks ago you've been assaulted by a crackpot and keelhauled by a wild animal, and your girlfriend told you to drop dead. Then you attacked your best friend breaking your own nose and dislocating your little finger. Your karma is in a seriously retro phase. Not to mention your compos mentis. Nobody in their right mind tackles a bear."

"I did not *tackle* a bear, Miranda, it tackled *me* when I fired my gun in the air."

"Can you hear yourself, Dad? Do you understand what you're saying? Does your behavior, by chance, seem a bit ludicrous to you upon reflection?"

Yes, I could hear myself loud and clear. Of course I understood what I was saying. I agreed absolutely that my karma was in a retro phase. Ditto my face. For sure I was headed for an appointment in Samarra if I couldn't rein in my Mr. Hyde persona. And so—?

So "I'm healed," I said, inspecting my hands and the cast on my arm through the eye that wasn't swollen shut. "We are going to summit Spoon Mountain tomorrow. Period. Exclamation point. End of discussion."

Lizzy said, "If Poppy wants to climb the mountain you should let him. He's a grown man. He's older and wiser than everybody else here."

"Bag it, sugar," Miranda said. "If we want your opinion we'll ask for it. Little kids should be seen not heard."

"I am not a little *goat*," Lizzy protested. "I have rights too. I am not some kind of drooling animal that—"

Michael frowned at Lizzy, putting a finger to his lips: "Shh." For some reason Lizzy took the hint as they all fell silent eyeing me askance while I glowered at them sadly . . . and defiantly. Cujo snored. Having awaited the opportunity all night, Jamie could hold back no longer—she sneezed. And immediately *her* Mr. Hyde persona commented: "If you ever changed the litter in that cat box people might be able to breathe."

Though I wanted to reply with a scathing comeback I resisted the urge. The hole I was digging was deep enough. I wanted Ben on my side tomorrow. I wanted him up high with me and Miranda. I wanted him to break the law and share an epiphany with us on top of Spoon Mountain. And carry me back to safety if I collapsed. Trashing Jamie was not an option. So I held my fire.

Miranda blew her nose onto a paper towel and remained calm. "You have to give it up, Dad, no eleventh hour hero-ics. Better to eat humble pie. Look at you, you can't even survive at this altitude let alone at twelve thousand feet." She reached over to playfully tweak my enormous nose; I jerked my head away. "We are not climbing that moun-tain with you tomorrow because we love you too much," Miranda concluded. "I'm sorry, it just isn't right."

"Yes it is. We used to climb all the time in the old days. We promised each other."

Miranda stood up and went behind me, leaning to circle her arms around my shoulders as she pressed her cheek against the side of my wounded head. "Poppa, we adore you, doesn't that make any impression on your addled bean? You're funny, you're a flake, and you're a cool human being. We even respect your nonsensical stubborn behavior against all the odds because compared to most people at least you have guts. However, we don't want to lose you yet."

I thought about that. I didn't want to lose them either. But we would get nowhere talking about how much we loved each other. Frankly, I was drowning in panic. I mean it, I was really scared. It's not as if we had forever. How could my children be so obtuse? Sometimes you have to seize the day before the opportunity dissolves . . . otherwise, heaven forbid, you might wind up pampered and comfortable and well fed during your golden years safely ensconced in the bosom of your family, all of whose members respect you and kowtow to your every aging need and whim with ultra-solicitous tenderness and boundless adoration. And what sort of lily-livered Lilliputian desires a fairy-tale ending like that?

Ergo? In typical fashion I unsheathed my razor-sharp kendo sword and committed seppuku. I accomplished this by uttering words that made no sense. I said, "At least *I* am climbing that mountain tomorrow. And nobody is going to stop me."

My lovely daughter straightened up, catching me by surprise. She dropped her gloves right in the middle of our hockey game and said, "Okay, Dad. Come on guys. Let's bail on this punk."

"Whoa," Ben said. "Take it easy, Miranda."

"You take it easy, Ben. Come on everybody, time's up. I've listened to enough BS. I'm turning into a pumpkin."

"Oh hey, wait a sec," Michael said. "Let's not go bananas. It's your dad's birthday. He's sixty-five years old. We didn't come here to—"

"To hell with his birthday," Miranda said. She was looking straight at me. In all the years we had gone toe-to-toe I had never, to my recollection, seen such fury in her eyes. Call it a combination of love, hate, anguish, frustration, hopelessness—name an emotion. Overriding everything was an aura of being utterly fed up. At long last my straw had broken her camel's back. It was finally time for Miranda to honestly kick me in the groin, giving me what I honestly deserved. Oblivious me, I guess I had crossed the line.

"My dad is a fool," Miranda said. "He's a joke. I'm sick of all his self-righteous treacle and his lugubrious self-annihilation complex for the last thirty years. Where was he when we needed him? I know why he wants to climb Spoon Mountain tomorrow and I sympathize with his desire but frankly I don't give a rat's ass if he murders himself doing it because he is in no condition to succeed. We made a promise to each other? Spare me. This isn't twenty years ago and I'm not a little girl anymore. I'm a nurse, I have skills and knowledge, and somebody has to be responsible. Let Ralph Nader speak at his funeral, *I went fishin'.*"

Ben waved his hands. "No no, what are you doing? We can't let the party end this way. She apologizes, Pop, she doesn't mean it do you, Mandy?" My son cast about desperately. Though he did not want me to climb tomorrow, he had no wish to destroy my party, either. "Look, nobody even finished their food," he said. "There's all this food we didn't eat—"

"Let *him* finish the food, Ben." Miranda grabbed Lizzy's hand and headed for the exit. "And I hope he chokes on it. I hope his LDL cholesterol goes through the roof and blows out his arteries tomorrow. I hope Spoon Mountain eats him alive and poops out his bloody remains. Why should I apologize to that narcissist? He has never apologized to us. Come on, Michael, let's ditch this grubby hole before the sanctimony gives me an aneurism."

"Wait!" Ben said. He waved his hands some more. Ben *never* waves his hands. "You better stop this, Miranda. This isn't funny. What are you doing? You're not being reasonable. Or responsible. This is our father. It's his birthday. And you're acting like a . . . like a . . . you're acting like a . . ."

Ben floundered, searching for a word until at last he blurted ". . . *prima donna!*" like a man crying "*Fore!*" on a golf course. The minute he said it he regretted it. Even a fish wouldn't get caught if it kept its mouth shut. Ben froze as if he'd been spotted by a prison searchlight beam spreadeagled like a lizard halfway up a chain-link fence topped by razor wire.

Miranda contemplated her brother, incredulous, hesitating for only half a beat before dropping Lizzy's hand, sitting back down, and lighting into Ben:

"'Prima donna?' Who are you calling a 'prima donna,' Ben? Where did you learn such a big word? I'm impressed.

And I'm not 'reasonable?' I'm not 'responsible?' Are you crazy? I have been the only grown-up in this family since I was four. I have looked after you your entire life because you couldn't tie your own shoelaces without falling backward into a bucket of slops. You are never going to grow up and neither is our dad. I don't hold that against you and believe it or not I don't even hold it against the old man because he can't help himself. He was born crippled."

Jamie raised her hand like a kid in class. "Ben can *so* tie his own shoelaces," she said. "And he is a heckuva lot more dignified than you've ever been. Where do you get off insulting your big brother who never did you an inch of harm?"

"I'm not 'insulting' my big brother, Jamie. I can say whatever I want to about Ben because I love him and he understands. We grew *up* together. I took *care* of him."

Jamie said, "I love him too, and just because he never complains does not mean people can't hurt him to the core."

"Our dad is not 'crippled,'" Ben mumbled, red-faced and trembling. His head had been jerking back and forth between Miranda and Jamie in parody of watching a tennis game. "We shouldn't be mean to him on his special day . . ."

"He is *so* 'crippled.'" Miranda pushed up her sleeves to give her arms more gesticulating room. She was pissed off. "Lizzy, go outside and play with a moonbeam, we'll be there in a minute. Ben, I don't hold grudges, what's the point? But nobody on earth has been less 'reasonable' and less 'responsible' than our father. So don't you hand me that bogus 'prima donna' crap. He is totally inept in real life because he has been trapped in his little-boy imagination from the git-go and he doesn't know how to escape from the spell of his own looking glass. And now, apparently, he is eager to sodomize himself, and therefore the rest of us, by climbing a thirteener alone tomorrow with a broken nose, a broken arm, a black eye, a potbelly, and a serious heart condition."

"Hey, watch it, what kind of language is that to use in front of our daughter?" Michael raised *his* hand. "Why don't you tone it down a couple of notches, Miranda?"

"Oh shut up, Michael. You stay out of this. It's not your battle. Lizzy, go to the other room, play with the cats, turn on the TV."

"No, I've got as much right to speak here as you do," Michael said. "I am part of this family. And Ben is correct, you *are* a prima donna, at least you've acted like a prima donna by putting down your dad ever since we got married and I have always been uncomfortable with that."

Miranda held up her right hand, rubbing the thumb and index finger together ten inches in front of Michael's face. "You know what this is, honey? It's the world's tiniest violin."

"Jeepers, you are so *condescending*," Jamie said. "You should be ashamed of yourself, Miranda."

Miranda swung her finger to point directly at Jamie. "One more word out of you," she warned. "Go ahead, I dare you. Don't tempt me. *Just one more word.*"

"Wait a minute," Ben said, starting to point his accusatory finger at Miranda. "Wait a minute, this is my girlfriend you're insulting . . ."

"No, she's not insulting Jamie," Michael said. "Relax,

Ben. Mandy, I love you and I think you're perfect, too. But I don't enjoy how you bully your dad and it's high time I spoke my mind about this."

"No it isn't," Miranda said. "You're opening the wrong door into the wrong room for the wrong reasons."

Michael soldiered on anyway. "Your dad has never deliberately hurt you that I can see. And I have to say I do not understand why you rag him so much, a person with your profound concern for other human beings. It's as if a magic wand turns you into a fishwife whenever you're with him."

Miranda opened her mouth to nail her errant husband but Ben got there first.

"Wait a minute, Michael," Ben said. He shifted his finger to point at Michael. "Let's don't be saying rude things to my sister, okay? What is a fishwife? You should back off and say you're sorry, okay?"

"No, don't go there, Ben. Please." Jamie latched onto Ben's left arm with both hands. "You're not good at this sort of thing."

Miranda agreed. "That's right, my brother. Words to the wise. Heed her and leave Michael alone, he's an amateur, he's not even firing BBs at me. The issue here is not me, it isn't Michael, it is our demented father who—"

"He is not *demented*," Michael interrupted. "Miranda, you are so unfairly prejudiced against your own father it's terrible. I'm shocked. You're usually a rational and forgiving person."

"'My own father?'" Miranda reached into a serving dish for a stalk of broccoli and flung it at Michael. It ricocheted from his shoulder and knocked off Lizzy's baseball cap. Ben flinched and Jamie gasped. Lizzy had not moved since being ordered to leave the room, go play with a moonbeam, or turn on the TV.

"What do you know about my own father, Michael?" Miranda said. "My own *father*? I'll tell you something about my own father. First of all, I am a decent human being. That means I don't jump people simply because I was born priapic . . . like my own father. And I don't mock them in over-the-top childish left-wing novels I write . . . like my own father. And I don't blow all my money on frivolous tarts in platform heels with big knockers . . . like my own father. And I don't run around in a clown outfit gobbling Viagra crying 'The Arctic is melting! The Arctic is melting!' like my own father. Furthermore, in case you hadn't noticed, he's got our daughter speaking in tongues, in *raven* tongues no less, for God's sake. He doesn't have any boundaries. He used to wear a Mao cap covered by Baby Lenin pins he bought wholesale from a commie distributor in Brooklyn. You know what *Publishers Weekly* called the last novel he published? 'Utter juvenile bedlam.' They were being charitable. Have you ever even read one of his later-period books? It's like watching a house you just finished building get hit by a wrecking ball."

"Wait a minute," Ben said, pointing his finger back at Miranda. "You can't . . . I mean . . . it isn't . . ."

"Excuse me for another damn minute," Michael said, ignoring Ben. "I resent that, Miranda. I have read at least three of his books and they are great. They are funny. They make me laugh. They are sardonic and satirical and filled with universal truths and it wouldn't hurt you to recognize and understand that fact if you weren't so pigheaded and prejudiced and so full of—"

"Don't talk to my sister like that," Ben said. He pushed up from his chair and leaned over the table toward Michael with one hand now cocked in a threat position. Jamie said, "Ben, stop, you're not in control of yourself." Ben's face was really flushed. Lizzy tossed the broccoli stalk back at her mom, missing by a mile. Nobody noticed.

"Oh for Christ's sake," Miranda said. "Zip it, Ben. Sit down or take a walk around the block with your uptight girlfriend and mellow out. Lizzy, I asked you to leave this room, please. And as for you, Michael, you don't know fuck-all about what goes on in the tormented psychic bowels of a truly dysfunctional family. So don't cross this Rubicon, darling. You're treading on really thin water—"

"No I'm not," Michael interrupted again. "I happen to also be a member of this family and I *like* your dad. He has more brains than most people I know and a rich imagination. If we didn't have people of his ilk to amuse and inform us it would be a drab world. So get off of your high horse, you asshole, and quit dumping on your dad."

Ben shivered top to bottom and was about to paste Michael when Lizzy blurted, "Why is everybody *swearing*? You people always tell me I'm not *supposed* to swear! But right now all I am hearing from you guys is *swear* words all over the place! You're crazy as a bunch of *bedbugs*!"

"We are not 'you people,' or 'you guys,'" Miranda said calmly. "And we are not 'a bunch of bedbugs,' either. We are your parents, young lady, and I asked you to go outside or go watch TV and you have completely ignored me. So I'm going to count to ten and then—"

"Leave Elizabeth alone, she's innocent," Michael said. "I can't believe it, Mandy, but you have gone completely off the deep end. You are such a putz."

Ben, preparing again to punch Michael, was deflected, again, by Lizzy: "I *love* Poppy!" she shouted with her eyes closed and her fingers balled into fists. "He's funny! He never talks down to me! He treats me like a real human being! You guys *never* treat me like a real human being! You treat me like I'm a nobody! But I'm not a nobody, I'm a real person! *I hate the Pittsburgh Steelers!*"

"We know you're a real person," Michael informed Lizzy. "This is not about you so don't get excited. This is about your mom attacking Poppy for no good reason except that—"

"Enough," Miranda interrupted. "You are walking right into the mouth of the lion and you don't want to go there, buster. 'Putz?' You're going to regret that until hell freezes over. Lizzy, come here, don't be afraid, pretend we're all just playing Halloween. Meanwhile, program this thought into your thick skull if you can, Michael, and then click the save button: I love my dad but that doesn't mean he's not a retard. Capeesh?"

"Wait a minute . . ." Ben groaned, teetering on the brink of meltdown. "Our dad is not a retard, Mandy . . ."

"I told you to *sit*, Ben. Take a load off, *now*."

Ben sat down with a plop.

Michael said, "For chrissakes you can't call your dad a 'retard,' Miranda. I'm shocked and I'm—"

"You're *busted*," Miranda interrupted. "I'm grounding you for a month and taking away your homecooked meals and your sex privileges and if you think I'm kidding even one tiny iota I'll hire a lawyer to back me up, that's a promise. Lizzy, come here, that's an order."

Lizzy went over and climbed into her mom's lap. Miranda smoothed Lizzy's hair, "There there, dear." Lizzy's face was not wet, it was defiant. Michael's features appeared to have been rearranged by a stun gun.

"We should respect Pop," Ben said hoarsely, fighting back tears. "Isn't he our dad? Tonight is his birthday party. He's sixty-five years *old*, Mandy. Why are you doing this to our family?"

Miranda cupped her hands over Lizzy's ears so she would not hear the upcoming tirade: "Our family? What *family*, Ben? This family is a laughingstock. Our mother is still putting in seventy-hour workweeks to prove she has bigger balls than Long Dong Silver. And our *father*? Lord love a duck. My whole life I'm terrified Dad is going to burn himself with matches, emigrate to the Soviet Union, impregnate Anna Nicole, or give all his money away to the Julio Cortázar Hospital Fund in Nicaragua. He is a very unstable person who, after divorcing our mom, married a schizophrenic slut with three deranged kids, lost everything to them in the next divorce, then hooked up with an oversexed B-movie 'actress' who left him two years later for an IQ-challenged rodeo cowboy, and after that he fell in love with a local policewoman who won a karaoke contest singing Tom Jones songs at the El Patio Bar and Grill the week after she took a wet T-shirt competition at Ogilvie's.

Our *father.* And he calls himself a Marxist? Who does he mean—Groucho? Harpo? Chico? Zeppo? Me, I spend four nights a week on twelve-hour shifts praying my patients won't turn into vegetables because I caught the family disease of total ineptitude when I was too young to defend myself. Until tonight I used to thank God that at least Michael and Lizzy were real people from planet Earth who didn't even do drugs or watch *American Idol,* but now I'm not so sure. All of us in this 'family' communicate with each other maybe once per annum, max, on a good year, and, if memory serves, this is the first birthday we've shared with our dad in a quarter century. So quit living in a fantasy, Ben. And you just watch me take a walk from this bogus birthday party, you obsequious goody two-shoes. You crybaby. Stop sniveling. You don't have the spine of a jellyfish and you can't blame it on diabetes. Quit hugging him, Jamie, you'll suffocate the poor boy, you'll kill him with your vicious kindness. Ben, you slump around like a mute with your silent-waters-run-deep persona hoping to ingratiate yourself with our so-called father to gain his love and approbation but I have news for you, kiddo—lots of luck. When are you ever going to grow up and realize our so-called father is a charlatan, a burned-out scoundrel, a con man, a fuddy-duddy, an imposter, a phony lefty, a serial gigolo and a—"

I jumped to my feet bawling, *"Get out of here, Miranda, I'm sick of your shit!"*

"Gladly!" she yelled back at me. *"It's about fucking time!"*

Cujo yowled until Jamie ordered *"Be quiet!"* so loudly the dog cowered, belly against the floor.

A chaotic flurry ensued. Miranda, Michael and Lizzy hustled out the kitchen door, Lizzy hollering in dismay, "*I love you, Poppy!*" and Michael bleating, "*I'm sorry this happened, we apologize!*" and Miranda contradicting him, "*The hell we apologize!*" Before she was out of sight Lizzy tossed some flustered raven calls at me and I responded to her in baffled sympathy: "*Klek! Klek! Klek!*" Jamie tugged Ben up and shoved her hand through his arm in an effort to pull him away, too: "Ben, please, let's escape this madhouse." He resisted, shrugging her off so roughly that she stumbled against the refrigerator.

Yikes.

Ben had a bewildered, heartbroken look as if he should have been the man in our family who could save everybody with his forceful attitude and wise decisions, thus averting a debacle. Too bad—the world had crumbled all around him anyway and he had been unable to halt the carnage. Ben was big and strong, and he was a decent human being and a hard worker, and he was honest to the core. Too, he loved his sister and his father and his girlfriend and his niece and his brother-in-law and even his large, imbecilic dog, yet that had made no difference at all. Welcome to adulthood, son, and, if it's any consolation, I'm sorry. Learn to live with it.

Then, when Ben's eyes met mine, *I* flinched. First Sally, next Miranda, now Ben. When it rains it pours. I certainly have a way with people. And to top everything off, fuming and humiliated Jamie could not resist castigating me into the bargain:

"Are you *happy* now?" she sneered. "Are you *satisfied*?

Is this what you *wanted*? Does it feel *good*? Have you proved that you're a big tough *man*? And do you enjoy destroying every—"

"Shut up, you Nazi," Ben said and slapped her.

Twenty-nine

L isten to this:

When Miranda turned ten, Ben was twelve years old. Miranda was popular, she had many summer friends and they all attended her birthday party. Ben had only one summer friend that year, a boy named Stuart Driscoll. Stuart's dad was in jail and his mother was a lush. Her name was Charlene and, briefly, I found her attractive. We drank and smoked dope together and rioted between the sheets. Through us Ben and Stuart connected. I don't know what their relationship was based on. Loneliness, perhaps. They were mysterious boys. They sat in our crab apple tree for hours talking to each other. Or I think they were talking. Sometimes they walked around the back field hitting the tall grass with woolly mullein stalks. They were aimless and inseparable. Stuart Driscoll did not play sports or attend Cub Scout meetings or carry a pocketknife. He was about half Ben's size and wore glasses. He had buckteeth and a high, shrill voice. He was a nerd who did not play chess or read grown-up books. His mother told me, "Stuart is a sweet kid who doesn't have a brain in his body." Stuart and Ben remained pals during my fling with Charlene straight to the end of that summer.

Miranda's birthday is in August so we always celebrated it at my house on Upper Ranchitos Road before I lost the house in my second divorce. Actually, the year Miranda turned ten we organized her party alongside the Río Grande south of town in a recreation area where the BLM has picnic tables, cabanas, and barbecue pits. Ben was happy that Charlene brought along Stuart. Miranda hated Stuart, who knew why? Maybe simply on general principles, though I believe my daughter had deeper cavils. She was not an unfairly judgmental kid. Years later I tipped that it must have been because she despised Charlene. I am a slow study.

We had a rambunctious summertime fiesta beside the wide river where the fish were jumping and the cottonwoods (and some of the adults) were high. Charlene and several other parents helped me distribute the soda pop and cook up hot dogs and hang a piñata from a tree branch and keep track of children in the water. The river flows slowly in that place and was almost clear, with shallow areas and sandbars. But you can't be cavalier around the Río Grande. Kids were forbidden to wade out too far toward the main current. In her skimpy bikini Charlene was a provocative physical specimen splashing among them keeping tabs.

I was watching my lover and Miranda and her giddy friends playing a game they had invented with balloons called "water slaughter" when Stuart Driscoll appeared in front of me. He asked, "What's the matter with Ben?"

Ben? I looked around and could not see him. "What do you mean?" I asked. "Where is he?"

Stuart pointed. "He's over there."

Oh no. I ran to a nearby cabana where Ben was back in the shade sitting alone matter-of-factly on a concrete bench slumped against the picnic table wearing a T-shirt and his bathing suit. He was out of it, already in shock. I don't know what had happened. Did he shoot up but then forget to eat in his excitement over the party? He was not wearing his fanny pack with the insulin paraphernalia and granola bars. He had taken it off to go swimming or forgotten to bring it along, and I had not checked beforehand. It was nowhere around. Afterward Ben could not remember. We never located the fanny pack.

I panicked and forgot what to do. Ben did not respond when I shook him. I stuffed a bun in his mouth; he was too woozy to chew or swallow. Miranda appeared, saying, "Give him this." She splashed Dr. Pepper from a bottle between his lips but it didn't work, it bubbled out. I ran to the car for my kit which wasn't there either. Incredibly, I had left it at home. Really? "You have to be kidding!" I yelled, turning the car upside down in frantic seconds, an act that was a crazy waste of time as Miranda and two parents brought Ben to the car. "Let's go, hurry up," my daughter said as they wrangled him into the front seat and she jumped in back. "Come on, Dad, step on it!" I gave orders for the other grown-ups to round up the kids and ferry them to town and then I left that place, driving desperately over eighteen terrible miles to the hospital while Miranda leaned over the seat hugging her brother and swearing, "Don't you fuck around, Ben. Don't you fuck around with us." That must have been the first time I heard the F-word from her mouth. When she tried to jam a cupcake into Ben he choked causing it to crumble everywhere except down his gullet. Nobody had cell phones in those days.

Obviously, Ben survived. His mother went to Child Protective Services and then decided to sue me in court to end my shared custody of Ben and his sister. I forget the legal terms she used. I was "irresponsible," "inattentive," "untrustworthy," "lacking in common sense," and guilty of placing Ben "in jeopardy of serious bodily harm." I felt so remorseful I would have thrown in the towel without a peep if Miranda had not urged me to resist. "You're our dad," she said. "If you crumple we'll feel bad. We love Mom, but you are not deliberately a moron, is he, Ben? Ben, my lips are moving I'm *talking* to you."

Ben shook his head emphatically.

"Say it out loud," Miranda said.

"Say what out loud?" Ben looked really uncomfortable and trapped.

"That he's not deliberately a moron," Miranda coached.

"No he isn't," Ben said, nodding more emphatically.

After pulling the plug on Charlene Driscoll I hired a lawyer to fight back. I had Hollywood money from a project for HBO that never got a green light. My children refused to help their mother's lawyer build a case against me. That was a bad time for all of us. Miranda insisted, "We're not taking sides, we just want to be ordinary deprived children in an ordinary broken family with an ordinary dopey mom and an ordinary dopey dad. Even a half-baked dad is better than no dad at all."

In due course, their mother dropped the court case but insisted on mediation through Child Protective Services and a parenting agreement. I was required to do a urine analysis each week the kids were with me to prove to her I was not drug impaired. I signed the agreement and Ben never had another crisis of low blood sugar while under my watchful gaze. And he never held Miranda's tenth birthday party against me either, poor baby. But he will now, I predict. It's a whole new ball game.

Thirty

Who knocks on my door at six a.m.? I opened my one functioning eye, unsure if I had heard correctly. Then I waited, groggy, only a quarter awake. To say that my head ached would be like saying Sandy Koufax could pitch. There came another rap rap, softly rapping on my kitchen door. Not bold or emphatic or in any way aggressive. Didn't sound like the cops or perhaps a chubby sweat-stained court functionary hoping to deliver a subpoena. Or what about my former pal Roberto Salazar bent on revenge? Violence begets violence which begets more violence. You're nobody until *everybody* hates you.

I waited out another respectable pause until one more knock was given. My bedside digital alarm clock said 6:05. On either side of me Cookie and Carlos had raised their heads. Then they slunk into my closet, just in case. The outdoors world was quiet. I heard a mourning dove and some magpies far away. Would whoever it was at my door kindly split? Or could it possibly be that either Ben or Miranda or both of them had returned. To apologize? Doubtful. To see if I was all right? Maybe. Chances were, however, that they wanted, in no uncertain terms, to quash my hike today.

The idea that either of them might be on my kitchen stoop spurred me to action, eager for reconciliation. Maybe it wasn't too late. Perhaps a spark still glowed among the embers that I might rekindle before they crossed me off for good. I thrust aside the covers swinging my legs off the bed and sat for a spell gathering what might pass for strength. A vertigo blip came and went. Next, I managed to stand upright with only muted cries of anguish as my knees and spinal column crackled. Bless old bones. My broken nose throbbed. Pulling on a pair of trousers, I shuffled into the kitchen and opened the door prepared to promise anything if only they would give me one more chance to make amends.

Mistake number one. There stood Don the Man, his legs belligerently spread, gripping his baseball bat crosswise against his chest like a union thug on the Jersey docks ready to bonk the head of a scab. I immediately sensed that he'd forgotten to take his ADHD medicine today. *Oh why hadn't I pressed charges?*

"Hi," he said, speaking with a slight southern accent. "May I come in?"

Did I have a choice? "I guess you can enter if you want," I said. Mistake number two.

"If I 'want?'"

"Okay, sorry. Come on in, please."

"My pleasure." Once inside he glanced with mild disapproval at the disorder from last night. I hadn't washed any dishes or cleared the table. Two chairs were tipped over. Miniature red, white, and blue candles decorated my birthday cake. His eyes were bright blue. A silver cross twice the size of my bulbous nose dangled around Don's neck. You can't laugh off Catholicism's ability to deform tiny minds.

"Seems that you had a party, old sport." Don tapped the barrel of his Louisville Slugger against the sink counter on which were piled dirty plates, glasses, pots and pans, silverware. "What happened to your face? Is the puta in attendance by any chance?"

"No, she broke up with me. But she's not a puta, she is a vibrant, independent, and intelligent woman."

Mistake number three. You don't argue with a person of Don the Man's unlimited cognitive dissonance while he is brandishing a baseball bat.

Don said, "My wife is so vibrant and independent that she's letting you use her for sex and then you'll abandon her because you've got a heart like a stone, everybody agrees, you dirty Red. You have about as much genuine compassion as a flea on a cat, that's your reputation and I do not take kindly to it."

"She's not your wife," I replied bravely. "You guys were divorced years ago. She is a free woman."

"Oh yeah?" Don the Man stepped forward, squared himself, and swung his baseball bat smashing everything off the counter beside the sink filling the air with a slow-motion maelstrom of fractured glass, ceramic plate pieces, knives, forks and spoons, linguini strands, mussel shells, broccoli bits, arugula leaves, and assorted pots and serving utensils. Crap splattered everywhere taking forever to get there. Then he changed his stance and whopped the birthday cake, blasting it so emphatically apart that the entire kitchen, including myself, was instantly plastered by cake icing and sticky crumbs as if those gooey particles had been shot from the ejection chamber of a tree limb mulcher. A wine bottle bounced off my photograph bulletin board spraying red grappa across the wall, desk, floor, and bookcase. I had never witnessed such violence. Don's shillelagh was as destructive as two planes hitting the World Trade Center. I stood corrected.

"The *hell* she broke up with you," he said. "She's a sucker for heels and she'll come crawling back to you unless I stop you in your tracks because you'll ruin her *and* our boys if I let you."

"I doubt that," I said. "Sally doesn't crawl. She walks on her own two feet."

"That's an intelligent thing to say in your situation," he replied. "You must be thicker than I thought."

"I didn't realize you could think," I said. "And this is the thanks I get for not pressing charges against you?"

"That's your problem, not mine. I can't help it if you're a bleeding heart."

"Time for you to go," I said. "You've overstayed your welcome. I don't like you anymore."

"Too bad. I'm barely getting started, dude. I didn't stop by here to kiss and make up, that's for sure you purveyor of smut. All your books should be burned."

My adversary stood five-eight, he was muscular. He wore a *Semper Fi* T-shirt, cammy fatigues, and brown desert boots. I'm surprised there wasn't a ring of black stitches around his cranium and a wooden surveyor's stake piercing both temples. His handsome features were the spitting image of Brad Pitt's, those blue eyes, full lips, cleft chin. His thick blond hair twisted into Rasta pigtails suggested Styrofoam peanuts caught in a gerbil's exercise wheel.

Walking purposefully to the bedroom I retrieved my .22 revolver from the top bureau drawer and returned to the kitchen. Don stood exactly where I had left him, all set for our showdown. The aluminum splint on my left pinkie made it difficult to grasp the gun. Never mind, where there's a will there's a way.

"Make like a breeze and blow," I said. "Otherwise—"

"Otherwise, what are you going to do, shoot me?"

"If you don't leave, yes."

"Go ahead and shoot me, then." Fastidiously, he set his bat onto the table among a medley of cake crumbs, wine puddles, and broken dishes. "I dare you." Don raised the hem of his T-shirt up under his armpits exposing a torso that had obviously been sculpted at a gym. "I'm not afraid of your pop gun. You can't hurt me. I'm not like all the other doormats you've wiped your feet on before. God is on my side." His fists thumped against his pecs gorilla fashion. "Put a bullet in my breadbasket, you chauvinist creep. Empty the entire cylinder." He grabbed his crucifix and shook it at me as if I was Count Dracula. "And when you're finished I'm going to teach you a lesson you won't forget so that you'll never take advantage of innocent women and children again."

I pointed my pistol at him, pried back the hammer with my left thumb, took careful aim, said "Suck on this, you infidel," and fired. The explosion was *loud*. Smoke spurted in many directions. The bullet splintered Don's crucifix and he spun around against the sink, sliding sideways along the counter with one arm sweeping off whatever leftovers remained, then he pitched to the floor face down shot through the heart and dead as a doornail . . . *whomp.*

And that's when I woke up because the alarm had started beeping.

Thirty-one

Okay. "Let's go." Carpe diem.

You live by the sword you die by the sword.

My twenty minute R & R after the easy ninety minute hike from the wilderness parking lot to Gallegos Lake at eleven thousand feet was over, Rover, and I was out of organic raisins for the gray jays. "Beat it, freeloaders." They waited on nearby limbs staring at me, miffed, the way bums who washed my windshield in New York used to glare if I didn't tip them. It looked as if Miranda and Ben were not hustling up to search for me: Their tough love had called my bluff. So no more shilly-shallying. Standing, I muttered "Sayonara" to a dozen obedient tourists at the shrunken lake and retreated into spruce trees behind me, my heart fluttering from guilt. *Out of sight, out of bounds.* A bright red sign said: CLOSED DUE TO EXTREME FIRE DANGER—NO TRAVEL BEYOND THIS POINT. Screw the sign. Sick from fear, from the heat, from too much exertion already, I hobbled off through the evergreen shadows setting my trekking poles at every step, keeping balanced. A leather wrist strap held the sticks to my one hand with the cast and my other hand with the pinkie splint. That was awkward but I managed. At least my legs weren't broken. I drew in deep breaths to calm myself as I zigzagged among the trees, my temperature rising. Raggedy tufts of pastel green lichen beards dangled off all the branches. Layers of crisp needles covered the floor of the dark glade interspersed by islands of moss and withered leaflets so parched from the drought my every step crackled. I recoiled from the noise wishing a wind would rise to cover my tracks. "It's not going to happen," Miranda said. "You made this bed, now lie in it."

I was lying in it, believe me. You live an entire lifetime hoping for some kind of redemption and wind up right back at square one. How did that scene happen in my kitchen last night? What was it all about? Ben and Miranda and Michael and Lizzy and Jamie yelling not at me but at each other? Why do I *always* shoot myself in the foot? Despite the love I hold for my children I have shortchanged them repeatedly. No, I have not been deliberately unconscionable I don't think, I am just a self-centered superficial jackanape terrified of genuine affection. I've screwed up the logistics of my own existence so often that I never paid true attention to Miranda and Ben. They grew up mostly without me in the Capital City with their mother. When they needed me most I was in Hollywood, or gaga over a scintillating gold digger, or at a Million Man March in Washington D.C. Often when I phoned Miranda at her mother's simply to say "Hi," she would blurt, before I could mutter another word, "It's okay, Dad, I forgive you." Kids grow up fast. Their childhoods are erased in a blink. Your own life is a confused garble of work, politics, sickness and health, marriage and divorce, and too many wrong turns onto one-way streets for fatuous reasons. Children are a huge part of the deal, in fact they seal it. Look at Sally, she would never give up on her boys. Even Don the Man has more genuine emotional attachment to his ex-wife and to his kids than I do to mine. If you are otherwise preoccupied you miss the boat. Why am I so stubborn? Why did I order Miranda out of my house last night? Am I deranged? Why can't I hang Sally's picture on my kitchen wall without being goaded by a cattle prod? Who punches his one-legged best friend in the face? How could I process Ben's slap of Jamie? I *caused* it. I might just as well have assassinated the Archduke Franz Ferdinand. Does Lizzy think I'm crazy? Or, worse, a buffoon? What is the matter with me? What am I saving up for at sixty-five? *The train is leaving the station.* My whole life I've "walked the talk." I'm in favor of Justice, Equality, Liberty or Death. Read *The Lucky Underdogs* or *American Martyr* or *A Ghost on the Barricades.* I'm incorrigible; I make people laugh. There are even snippets of redeeming social value in *Bury My Heart at Peyton Place* and *The Bullfrog Diaries.* But who's laughing now? My private life is a washout, I've become a cartoon. My career is moribund. I wanted to climb Spoon Mountain *with* Ben and Miranda. As a gesture. An apology. A plea for our future. A salute to a promise made in our past. And to bring us together before I croaked. To show where I want my ashes dispersed. I don't even know, I'm confused, I'm *mortal.* It was an impromptu decision based on fear, love, yearning, hope. What *are* my motivations? I am frightened, for God's sake. My fear is personal and it's planetary. I want to lead Miranda and Ben, lead *us*, back to Eden. *Rewind history, please.* And our plan segued into just another test of wills because they are concerned for my well-being, they don't want their father to die, what's wrong with that? Why can't I allow them to *care* for me? I should be grateful for their vigilance and *devotion*. Is it wrong to let yourself be *loved*? I should turn around right now and go home and dial Miranda's cell phone to invite her for supper tonight at the Sagebrush Inn. Then I'll follow her advice, go on a diet, exercise. I'll do a treadmill test that says I'm okay. Eventually, she and I and Ben will climb Spoon Mountain together, same as in the old days. *With our knapsacks on our backs.* Maybe even before I can apologize and invite Miranda to supper she will say, "It's okay, Dad, I forgive you. You're my favorite oxymoron." Then I will call Ben: "Please absolve me, son, for causing that holocaust on my birthday." And down the road we'll arrange another birthday dinner. This time I will do it right. I'll make amends. I'll invite Roberto Salazar and Aaron Osborne to my party, I'll kiss their feet in expiation, I'll wait on them hand and foot. "All is forgiven, Roberto." "Allow me to pay for the damages, Aaron." Michael I will embrace, too, and praise him for going to bat for me last night. When it's finished I'll dedicate the Magnum Opus to him, who else? He has actually read *three* of my "satirical" books? He thinks I have "brains and a rich imagination?" Oh Michael. My son-in-law the plumber? I had no idea you were such a *fan*. And Smith's can bake me an unbirthday cake for his daughter Lizzy to prove I think she's a human being. A *wonderful* human being just like her father. I will entreat Sally to attend the party and ask her to marry me for reals this time around even though I *know* marriage is a capitalist plot in a patriarchal evangelical-driven society to define property and inheritance, nothing more. Doesn't matter. Engels, schmengels. I'll go to therapy with Sally and Jason. I'll beg Don the Man's pardon for not loving his ex-wife as she deserved. I'll send flowers to Jamie and then order Ben to marry her and if he refuses . . .

Thirty-two

Beyond the initial zone of "illegal" forest, out in the open, ferocious sunshine magnified by the smoggy sky mugged me. I stopped, reeling, feeling senile. "Beam me up, Scotty, this is so lame." Facing me was a wide boulder field where some monster rocks were three to five feet tall and harsh rays glaring off them stung my swollen eye. *Why didn't I bring sunglasses?* "Because you're a 'putz.'" Those obstacles were ominous and without a trail through them. There were no trees, no other vegetation, only heaps of busted stone craving an opportunity to brutalize my puny limbs. "I'm on my own, I'm alone." And at that thought sweat spurted off my forehead like rats leaving a sinking ship. I don't *want* to be alone. I'm *lonely.*

For at least fifty yards while traversing the talus I was exposed to the gazes of snoopy government snipers enforcing the hiking ban a quarter mile below. All I could do by way of subterfuge was hunch over to make myself a smaller target. I had not actually seen any gun-toting feds at the lake, yet they may have been camouflaged as ordinary citizens sporting dirndls and lederhosen with Mac-10s stashed in their olive-green fanny packs. Breathing hard, I lumbered along at a hesitant pace expecting a fatal bullet at any moment—it was impossible to climb faster. I wobbled at every step, planting my pole tips at difficult angles. Talk about sitting ducks. Diverted by dire presentiments I miscalculated and banged a shin and *squealed.*

Nobody shot me, though. And in due course, halting to take stock, I finally mustered enough courage to glance up at the surroundings whereupon the true nature of my folly boggled my fruitcake brain.

Oh. My. God. Yes, I had been here before, remember? "I ate Spoon Mountain for breakfast." I used to tell Ben and Miranda, "What are you complaining about? This isn't a mountain, it's a molehill."

Sure. Famous last words. Because that was then and now everything *loomed.* I had shrunk to the size of an aspirin and the peaks had grown to the size of whales. Old age sucks. To the east Engelmann spruce trees decimated by budworms ringed what was left of Gallegos Lake and above the trees Gavilán Peak stood at over thirteen thousand feet, a stark resplendent cone rising to massive cliff walls and escarpments cleft by narrow chutes on top. I developed a crick in my neck from gaping at the summit. How did we climb it that day chasing Miranda to the crest? "Don't be a rabbit, be a turtle." Daunting slides of scree under the highest promontories reflected a dramatic light that made me sway, alarmed by the overwhelming grandeur. From Gavilán Peak a jagged ridge circled west bleeding avalanches of boulders and featuring large granite teeth and rocky crags leading to Needle Mountain's crest. After that, another rim of turrets, shale spills, and metamorphic spurs bent further west interrupted by three impregnable defiles until it reached Sentinel Tower, a protuberance with crooked chimneys and slanted blocks striating its face that was pure primeval anatomy. To the right of this intimidating configuration rose Cabrito Peak, bald on its pinnacle, with three avalanche gullies littered by dead trees dropping off the north side. And beyond skulked Spoon Mountain, which for the moment was hidden from view. Though it used to be only "a friendly little mountain," I pictured it now eager to pulverize me and spit on my mangled corpse if I dared to penetrate its sphere of influence.

"Sixty-five is not thirty-five, hotshot."

"Yeah," Ben said. The all-new Ben with *his* gloves off at last, the male-chauvinist barbarian Ben. "You're a feeble geezer now, Pop."

The basin offered unimpeded space on a heroic scale that might have struck me as magnificent despite all the adjectives required to describe it if I hadn't just become eligible for Medicare and been scared to death. Plus: If they caught me was it worth five thousand bucks and 60-point headlines across all the state blats to summit Spoon Mountain on my birthday? KEPLER CAPTURED BY COPS ABOVE TIMBERLINE! Hadn't the original idea been to climb with my children to prove I adored them and the natural world we live in?

"They'll hammer you to the cross, Dad," Miranda promised. "Mr. Political. Mr. Environmental. Mr. Hypocrisy Personified. They'll be all over you like a duck on a June bug."

"They'll put you in leg irons and manacles," Ben jeered. "Then smear on tar and feathers."

I had chewed off more than I could handle, the story of

my life. Have pity on me. I didn't know the gun was loaded. Yet after a few stutter steps in the wrong direction caused by my dim prospects I reversed myself and pushed forward because there was no other choice, was there? I had called my own bluff by initiating this enterprise in the first place, my usual modus operandi. And anyway, consider the alternative:

"Oh," Sally said, buffing her nails with an emery board. "You decided after all *not* to climb that mountain?"

Thirty-three

As I plodded higher I rested often. The lack of a man-made path to follow was not romantic, it was ter-rifying. I remembered Miranda scrambling ahead of us toward the top of Gavilán Peak. Then she would hit a wall and recover and scamper off again. Well, I had already hit a wall and could not recover. "Scamper?" What kind of a word is that? My baseball cap was soaked from perspiration, so were my shirt, pants, and knapsack. I guzzled water while leaning against a boulder as pitiless sunshine ate me alive. I tried taking my own pulse and gave up because it was racing *way* too fast. If I fainted now or kicked into ventricular fib—

Take it easy, warned my brain. *Don't be a rabbit, be a turtle.*

Grimacing, I wrapped the trekking pole handle straps around my wrists and progressed at a sluggish gait through a brief vein of spruce trees, a welcome relief of shadow that too soon gave way to the open again. I did not want to think about last night—anything but that. Why hadn't my son just shoved half a grapefruit into Jamie's face? Scuffing along a barren slope I arrived at a flat shelf and canvassed the panorama as I grappled for breath and emptied a second water bottle. I took a puff of Albuterol and stashed the inhaler back in my knapsack. Boulder slides tumbled from my feet in three directions; the perspective gave me vertigo. What perverted deity lacking intelligence had designed such bullying geology? My heart hiccupped and thumped so loudly that with my mouth open I could hear the erratic beats squish-squashing in my throat. "I'm exaggerating," I realized. To a younger person this outing would be a stroll through a summer meadow. Ben and Miranda, those nonchalant billy goats, had climbed these environs beside me with both hands tied behind their backs. "Last one to the top is a rotten egg!" We used to *sing* on the way up. We were *family*.

I peered with my lone functioning eyeball down through binoculars hoping that forest rangers led by a brace of federal bloodhounds had discovered my trail, yet no such luck. Maybe by now Miranda and Ben were hastening to save me? No, I could not locate them either, which also did not come as a revelation. It would've been so simple to have followed Miranda's advice, healing myself first, shedding twenty pounds, then doing a treadmill test. It would have been easy except that I was a narcissistic egomaniac in a clown outfit gobbling Viagra while the Arctic melted.

What happened in my kitchen last night?

I was lost, unhappy, once more without a clue. I fiddled with my camera and clicked off a few pictures to be remembered by. Twenty years hence, when they located my cryonically preserved remains imbedded in a glacier abutting Spoon Mountain's summit, the photographs might still be extant for my heirs to marvel over. Closing the aperture to f/16, I held the Nikon at arm's length in front of myself pointed back toward my own face and composed a giddy self-portrait of my grotesque features (black eye, puffy nose, torn lips), broken right arm raised, the fingers of my hand in a V sign with Gavilán Peak dominating the background. Come that future day Ben would kneel beside my half-exposed skull on which bleached tufts of ancient pelage were fluttering while Miranda rustled through the weathered knapsack:

"Hey Ben, look! Here's one of those antique cameras with a snapshot inside of our reasonable, responsible, and respected dad on his sixty-fifth birthday when he perished of heatstroke, a heart attack, and lethal naiveté combined."

"He got what he deserved," Ben said. "Good riddance to bad rubbish."

Thirty-four

Here's a tip straight from the horse's mouth. During moments of extreme duress you can mitigate the situation by deliberately daydreaming à la Dorothy from Kansas. It's a means of self-preservation. You take a deep breath, exhale, count to ten, and transport yourself to another world. And as I gained altitude I hied myself to an imaginary spot behind Bob's Diner from where I could observe my raven pals feeding on garbage at the two battered dumpsters near the back door. My granddaughter Lizzy was standing beside me studying the spectacle through her new binoculars, compliments of yours truly.

This is what we were looking at:

On days when the bins fill up with refuse many corvid gourmets arrive. They are iridescent black, larger than footballs, beady-eyed and abrasive. There can be fifteen or twenty at once taking turns jumping into the containers, pecking plastic bags or greasy donut boxes with their strong beaks. They'll empty the last cornflakes from Kellogg's cereal minis and drag lawn-and-leaf-sized sacks out onto the ground, methodically shredding them for decomposed strawberry pancakes, green chile omelets, lettuce leaves lacquered in ranch dressing, enchilada remains, refried beans, honey-covered sopaipilla chunks. While the feast takes place there is much jostling, hopping around, yawping, aggressive feather displays, courtship behavior, bill nibbling, and other pecking-order flare-ups that don't much interfere with the principal task at hand. The bullies shovel in more swill than the shyer birds, yet everyone salvages a few cold cuts or Cheerios from the operation. Alpha males strut about on the surrounding gravel with their heads held high, beaks open, "ear" feathers upraised and half-melted cheese strands dribbling out the sides of their mouths. Baby birds, fatter than their parents, crouch on the dumpster rims with quivering wings giving incessant screechy cries, begging to be fed. If they lived in apartment buildings Mom and Dad would shave off their pinion feathers and toss them out the windows.

Close your eyes and this carnival of lusty raven consumption could be a medieval jamboree replete with jousting, jesters, and caber tossing as burly Robin Hoods boasting enormous leather codpieces and bosomy Maid Marians laced tightly into their low-cut corsets tear the sizzling flesh off a spitted boar and toast each other with hot mead slopping over the brims of their gilded goblets.

Yessss.

Sally accompanied me only once on a birding expedition to Bob's Diner. She failed to see any beauty, complaining the show was voyeuristic, a pornographic gangbang and an environmental disaster. When I began to speak Raven she ordered me to quit. Right. Now. Because people in the vicinity would think I'm cuckoo. Sally is not as fascinated as I am, nor as my granddaughter Lizzy is, by the natural world. She does acknowledge that the glossy ravens are "handsome" and "bold." Nonetheless, viewing their undignified behavior at the receptacles fighting over restaurant discards turned her off.

"Who would want to spy on Queen Elizabeth while she's taking a dump?" Sally asked. She believes that Bob's Diner should contract with Waste Management, Inc. for brand-new refuse boxes sporting heavy metal lids. Thank God this would increase Bob's rent on the bins and he is a notorious skinflint when defending his profit margins. He can always hire an undocumented worker, cheap, to clean up after the birds (which is a downside of our town whose slippery-slope politics I won't address here). The ravens have no problem with Bob because they are implacable opportunists who will get into bed with anyone.

Lizzy has said to me more than once, "Poppy, I wish I had a whole room full of ravens every day to keep me company and talk with me." Only yesterday, before my birthday celebration blew up, Lizzy had suggested we build a bird blind behind Bob's Diner so we can observe the ravens more closely when she visits. "Over my dead body," Miranda countered. Lizzy wants a pet raven for Christmas. She would name it Taylor Lautner after a so-called hottie actor in the *Twilight* movie. Could she teach her pet raven, she wondered aloud, to say, "Tickle me, Elmo?"

"Sure," Miranda answered before I could open my mouth. "Or how about 'Polly wants a crack-up?'"

Ignoring my witty daughter, I do feel an urge to elaborate about Lizzy before this story is over. I want to fill in the important gaps. Possibly I should reedit the manuscript, inserting these comments toward the middle of the book, but I'm too tired. My horse has already left the barn.

First and foremost, hear this: Lizzy is on my side. The side I abandoned years ago and am so desperate to recapture. Lizzy doesn't think I'm a phony lefty or a Groucho Marxist. If Lizzy was high school age she would venerate Edward O. Wilson and Sue Hubbell. She likes beetles; she is not afraid of bees or tarantula hawks. We have chased butterflies together. I sent her painted lady caterpillars that she raised in her room. I gave her an ant farm for her sixth birthday. Who bought her the rats Wynken, Blynken, and Nod? *I* did. During her visit up north last autumn we collected sow bugs in my yard and stashed them in a terrarium. We drove out to the mesa and caught three lizards with a string loop rig on a fishing pole. We read about the insects, reptiles, and arthropods in my guidebooks. I have a hundred and seventy-three guidebooks, count 'em. Lizzy has her own western region guidebooks—to birds, reptiles, insects and spiders, butterflies, mammals, and flowers—that I have sent her the past two years. She gets a new one from me every Valentine's Day, Easter, Fourth of July, Halloween, Thanksgiving, Christmas, and of course on her birthday. Michael and Miranda tolerate these educational gifts, even if excessive: "It's his thing, let him do it, she'll survive." Lizzy is thrilled with each new acquisition. Though she can hardly read the descriptions she pores over the illustrations.

During one of my rare trips to the Capital City a while ago Michael and I built a bird feeder outside Lizzy's window. I'm guessing Miranda considered it a great improvement over large bins filled with garbage. Lizzy keeps the feeder stocked with wild bird seed, mostly millet and black oiled sunflower seeds her parents can buy at Smith's. I send her ten dollars a month for the purchases. Lizzy also has a small digital camera I gave her with which she takes pictures through her bedroom window of evening grosbeaks and house finches on the feeder. Angelina Aguilera's bowl has been moved from the windowsill to the top of Lizzy's bureau. Miranda and Michael have taught Lizzy how to download off the camera onto their computer and Lizzy can print the pictures by herself. Smart kid. I keep a file of the bird snapshots she sends me.

If I can help it Lizzy will not be the last child in the woods. She has invited her entire jump rope team to her house and those seven little girls will sit on her bed absolutely quiet while nibbling on organic jelly beans and following the action on the feeder. Miranda has described the scene for me in hushed tones over her cell phone. Lizzy whispers aloud the names of the feathered visitors and explains to her classmates if the visitors are migratory birds or year-round inhabitants and what kind of nests they build. It's not quite a grammar-school Audubon Society, but Lizzy is developing a reputation as "the bird girl" (and she doesn't even Tweet). She's not ashamed. Nobody thinks she is a geek or a nerd.

However, Lizzy and her jump rope pals are not allowed to listen to her Raven CD and squawk at each other for more than five minutes at a pop. "Somebody in this family," Miranda says, "has got to draw the line."

I call Lizzy My Talented Doppelgänger. It makes sense

that she has bonded with the dumpster divers behind Bob's Diner and is learning to speak their language off of that Raven CD, which, to Miranda's credit, I suppose, hasn't yet been melted accidentally atop a piece of raisin bread in the toaster oven. Miranda does not understand why my granddaughter isn't at all repulsed by birds wallowing in half-eaten chocolate éclairs and other tasty gunk. Like, how come Lizzy never says "Yuck"?

"I want to *be* a raven," Lizzy declares. Especially, she would like to perfect their "jumping jacks," hopping straight up and flapping her wings and bouncing when she lands straight back down again. "It's like prancing on the moon," she tells me. Her class recently saw a DVD about the first moon landing in 1969.

But according to Lizzy: "There's nothing *alive* up there. Everything alive is down *here*."

Thirty-five

And so the time passed as I traipsed aloft, head bowed, huffing noisily. Tap tap tap with the sticks; tappety tap. I was so stiff all my joints creaked, I groaned, I swore, often I teetered, disoriented, assessing the harsh landscape surrounding me with a swollen eye. In my day up here I had plowed through snowstorms on snowshoes, fearless and exhilarated. When Miranda grew tired on our summer excursions I would carry her pack along with my own. Yet now the hankering to desist, tuck tail, and escape gnawed more insistently than a marauding beaver. What I was doing was wrong. It made no sense. Who flees from those he loves in order to self-destruct?

I do. Like a salmon genetically programmed to kill itself I continued marching toward Spoon Mountain whose summit remained out of sight. Welcome to my world, fellow Rotarians. If it moves, fondle it. If it's insane, embrace it. If it is a book you are writing torpedo it with dim-witted hackneyed platitudes. I forged one step, another step, and trundled upward to the next talus spill where the jumbled stones were brown and gray and decorated by green lichens. They ridiculed me with a sheer indifference that I sneered at with phony swagger. Poo-tee-weet. I picked my way on tiptoes through the eerie terrain, me and my adjustable sticks, my little crutches. Then I pooched around a cliff peppered by stunted spruce trees clinging to fissures in the rock walls and ascended to a fallow ridge where I essayed four feeble steps at a time, pause . . . four more steps and pause again, my progress measured in nanocentimeters. It was agonizing. "Did you bring your ice ax and your pitons?" Sally giggled.

"Mock on, mock on, Voltaire, Rousseau."

Who knows how long it took me to advance above tree line? Nothing seemed familiar although I had passed this way before with my kids. That was long ago. They had not complained. All three of us had been born to travel *up*. We were young and strong. Ben rarely said a word but he liked to stop and train his binoculars on some distant rock pile or on a butterfly at our feet. "Come on, come on," Miranda urged, "we're a long way from the top." Ben did not care about the top. For him it was all about the journey. For his sister it was all about the goal. Between them both they licked the platter clean. Those trips were a gift I gave to them that you cannot take away from us. Or maybe you can. Where had they gone, the mountaintops and the porcupine tracks through snow, the falling of graupel on a summer afternoon and the song of a hermit thrush? All those things once flowed through our bones to give us purpose. Now they are faint shadows, scarcely evident. Who remembers what's important anymore?

I do. And so does my ex-best friend, Roberto Salazar. I remember walking through groves of golden-leaved aspens with Roberto on a September afternoon. I can see us on a fishing expedition leaping from one boulder to another while crossing the Río Grande, our legs splashed by the spindrift off white water. And I recall sitting beside my pal at a forest campfire listening to wind in the high ponderosa crowns.

"The thing is," Roberto told me, "you can't pretend animals don't think. They also have feelings like us. Animals grieve for their dead same as we do. Plants are more intelligent than people because they follow the plan no matter what. You can always count on animals and plants to do the right thing. La naturaleza manda. Nature rules."

We hunched over in the dark warming our hands around tin cups of cowboy coffee as the flames died. "Maybe I'm being sentimental," he appended, "but strike me dead if I am wrong."

I miss you, Roberto. And I'm sorry I punched out your lights even though you deserved it.

The sun was now located well west of overhead, its UV rays no doubt creating cancer cells by the score throughout my vulnerable body. The old days were never so torrid. At three-minute intervals I bent over, hands on my knees, relaxing until my heart subsided to a more tepid beat. I performed the Valsalva maneuver to restore a normal rhythm. How much more affliction could that fatigued muscle absorb before going haywire? Surrounding me— surprise!—lay another demolition derby of rugged boulders. I drank from one of my three remaining water bottles, imbibing a bizarre liquid that exited from all my pores simultaneously an instant after I swallowed it. Time to take a mulligan, pal, and return to the lunar module.

I stared at my cast. *Te quiero, güero.* "I love you, blondie."
Sure you do. The arm ached. Why hadn't I pressed charges?
My blackened eye ached. My lopsided nose ached. My entire
face ached. My brain ached, what was left of it. My pinkie
ached. My hemorrhoids were also cramping, an unpleasant
sensation. Top to bottom my flesh was consumed by pain. I
was light-headed, mumble-tongued, wooden-footed. How
can a person be so out of shape? It occurred to me that
I was committing suicide even though I did not want to
commit suicide . . . I don't think. My wristwatch indicated
that all told, starting at the wilderness parking lot, I had
been en route for three hours and nineteen minutes. "Look
at you," Miranda said. "You can't even survive at this altitude let alone at twelve thousand feet."

Ben said, "He's a has-been. He has always been a
has-been."

Fighting nausea I readjusted the trekking poles, short-
ening them up for steeper inclines. I inspected distant
ridgelines for the silhouettes of bighorn sheep tiptoeing
single file along a precipice. They were nowhere to be found.
I snapped another picture then glassed the lower slopes
searching for my children on their way to save me. But no
dice. Fancy that. I missed the company of Miranda and Ben
with a nagging, uncomfortable intensity. I wanted Sally
back, and I would embrace Alex and Zachary and Jason.
Whatever it took. "Boys, welcome to my home. Feel free
to crash my car. Steal my CDs. Stutter up a storm. Here's
a tube of lipstick. Rent tuxedos for the wedding." Roberto
will be my best man. Aaron can carry the ring on a petite
embroidered satin pillow. If I weaseled out of this adventure

alive would *my* children ever speak to me again? What happened in my kitchen last night? Ben slapped Jamie. How could he call Miranda a prima donna? I know he hates me now, I saw it in his eyes. He's turning into a werewolf. Is Lizzy afraid of me, too? Will she ever trust me again? I can't bear to lose her. She cried "I love you, Poppy!" on her way out. I can't get over the fact that Michael defended me. And he reads my books . . . but which ones? And why not the others? Why did Miranda yell those terrible things at Ben and Michael and Jamie? And without my children with me on this mountain what is the point anyway?

Human Anguish: Love it or leave it.

Thirty-six

You can't fight city hall and you can't stop progress, either. If you hang a bad dad on the wall in act one you have to destroy him by the end of the play.

As luck would have it I arrived at the base of a sharp incline of withered tundra grasses dotted by several dozen shrubby cinquefoil bushes barely two feet high and already brown rising to a saddle on a difficult ridgeline. The Saddle. I still could not see the top of Spoon Mountain. On either side of me the usual disconcerting cacophony of boulders was poised to dislodge and bound downhill, crushing me to a pulp. I cast my gimlet eye at the route pondering how the noted mountaineer/journalist Jon Krakauer would have described my predicament: *Then the tiny novelist adjusted his oxygen mask, double-checked the carabiner knots on his belay ropes, extended an aluminum ladder over the first crevasse, and jubilantly carried on toward the craggy wind-blasted summit of Spoon Mountain, the last of the planet's seven tallest peaks that he needed to bag in order to complete his alpine "grand slam," the reward for a lifetime of climbing adventures.*

I balked, wondering, *Where is the feasible line of ascent?* Miranda assured me, "There is no feasible line of ascent for the con man, the charlatan, the imposter, the serial gigolo."

Ben added, "He's also a joke, a fool, and a scoundrel." My baseball cap was wetter than saturated. My crotch was scraped raw from sweat. Had my watch stopped? No it had not. How long had it taken Lindbergh to reach Paris? When would delirium tremens commence?

Despite the drought I was surrounded by some vivid flower blossoms, few much larger than my thumbnail. To distract myself as I groveled higher I wanted to name them aloud, but could not remember. So Miranda remembered for me: "Alpine avens . . . moss campion . . . skypilot . . . Hayden's paintbrush . . ."

Oh what a smart little girl.

"Actually, she's a show-off," Ben corrected. "But we love her." He cackled.

How could such a variety of vegetation hold so tenaciously to this desiccated ground exposed to gale-force winds and the sun's harsh radiation? Incongruous butterflies appeared also—little yellow and blue ones and a small fritillary plus a handful of orange and black beauties called . . . what *were* they called?

"Milbert's tortoiseshells," Miranda said. "Everybody knows that."

Ben appended: "Everybody except *you*, Pop, you ignoramus."

"Stop it you two," I pleaded.

Pea-sized grasshoppers popped like popcorn against me, irritating buggers, very frenetic. And a marmot basking on a dusty outcrop whistled, announcing to its neighbors that a maladroit ape from the "civilized" world was invading their sacred space.

Thirty-seven

The ascent toward the Saddle eighty yards above was a nightmare. Picture a pitiful old fossil in need of an anti-inflammatory pill the size of an ostrich egg. In prep school I had run the mile and been undefeated my senior year in the 220 low hurdles. At fifty I had won the city parks B tennis championship for my age group. Years ago, Miranda and Ben and I had scurried up this slope as peppy as leaping lemurs from Madagascar. Those were the days. Now, at sixty-five, lungs burning, heart pumping out of sync, my face pummeled, my arm broken, my spirit sapped, I climbed on constant traverse, a dead man walking, five baby steps left, eight baby steps right, back and forth, slowly gaining altitude, resting every five yards rattled by the extreme effort required to maintain balance on the sharp incline. Had my principal diet for the past two decades been Chicken McNuggets and Pringles potato chips? The Valsalva maneuver failed to control my arrhythmias. I had a migraine. I was so baked my tongue had swelled. Needing to pee I was too tired to make the effort with my shriveled little penis. I could scarcely walk, waving my arms, often inching along on all fours grabbing handfuls of seared grass to steady myself. It was maniacal hard work in an ever thinning atmosphere where not a single cloud marked the polluted sky and the sun kept scorching the world. *Die, scum, die.* On the left more bare cliffs rose straight up; to the right chunks of rusty-colored rock were strewn from the ridgeline in landslides of jumbo "barnacles." Dead ahead lay my only route . . . where the contour lines on the geological survey maps grazed each other.

"Utter juvenile bedlam." Another pundit spewing venom for *Kirkus* had said I was, "Enamored of reckless tomfoolery." More pejoratives coined by the literary assassins have credited me with writing "pseudoradical puerility" and "infantile analysis." My later work has never lacked for defamatory reviews. *Harper's* once accused me of "Pandering to the gross tastes of drunken fraternity boys." Memorably, the *Anniston* (Alabama) *Star* called my last novel, "A feast for sore anuses." How did *that* get past their copyeditors? Insult to injury, Burrelle's Clipping Service sent me three copies of that disparaging screed, charging me triple what they should have.

If I could have sobbed I would have. Old age should rage. I wanted to escape this tragedy, I'm not King Lear. Who did I have to ball to get *off* of this mountain? I gathered myself to forge on, the spitting image of Rocky Balboa in the fourteenth round. Did Rocky ever throw in a towel no matter how severe his beating? No he did not. At least not until the director said, "Cut." Then he went to his air-conditioned trailer, showered off the fake blood, drank a Tanqueray and tonic, and had a delectable masseuse rolf his strapping body. My legs were weary, my feet sore, yet

I dragged myself uphill tussling against the heavy tug of gravity. Though the Saddle was not far, I might take forever to reach it. The air was dead calm. My bruised right eye throbbed; so did my fat nose and my cracked arm. And my ears were loudly ringing.

"Hello, Ben," I murmured, eager to hear a human voice. "Be reverent, son." My clamorous heart muffled my own words. "You're in nature's provenance now."

"You're always sweet to Ben," Miranda complained. "But you always snipe at me."

Ben said, "It's a dog-eat-dog world out there, Miranda. Learn to live with it."

Then he slapped her.

A stone's throw below the Saddle I sank to earth facing east toward Gavilán Peak across the basin. *No more, I'm finished.* I removed my cap, put it back on, swigged water and chewed on a handful of raisins then spit them out because they made me sicker. My ribs hurt, my calves quivered, my throat was constricted. I took another squirt of Albuterol. My heart boomed rapidly—buh-boom, buh-boom—and I was bloated from fatigue. Gallegos Lake had become a small blurry turquoise jewel only half the size it used to be, far away at the bottom of the alpine bowl. I glassed its shoreline for any tree cops peering aloft. Everyone had left the lake; it was deserted, nobody cared. That was an understatement. I was off their radar screens and could no longer count on an eleventh-hour collar to deliver me from my own worst instincts. And of course Miranda and Ben were nowhere in sight striding aloft to rescue me and proclaim their eternal devotion as they ferried their pathetic dad homeward strapped to a deerskin litter with a fringed sunshade over it.

"At least we're bringing him back alive," Ben said.

"No we're not," Miranda answered. "He's been dead for thirty years."

Bada boom.

Ben cackled again.

Thirty-eight

And this you are not going to believe, but it's true. My old friend Scarface, with his one tattered ear and an eye squashed into his socket, abruptly appeared below me on his way up toward the Saddle, intending, no doubt, to migrate over into the next watershed where a smattering of comestibles (despite the drought) and a dearth of people might be no small gift for a bear. Frankly, I was too tired to be surprised. In my condition things that don't make any sense made perfect sense to me. So why *wouldn't* the bear who had recently invaded my dumpster miles below this parched perch make another bizarre appearance in our story? After all, my karma was in a seriously retro phase.

That scrawny animal with one bloodshot eye and a fur coat mottled by mange and discolored by starvation waddled pigeon-toed up the slope directly toward me, his long snout nearly brushing against the earth. The beast did not halt until he smelled my odor. Then his head lifted and he sniffed, a curious gesture. Bears can't see very well out of two good eyes, let alone a single bad one. Scarface sat down ten feet below me and weaved his head slowly back and forth, analyzing me further I reckon, by scent. He did not seem perturbed although he was panting from heat and the effort of his travail.

"Ah, we meet again," is all I could say. "What are you doing up here?"

"I might ask you the same question," he replied aloud using impeccable English.

I know, I know. Talking animals is a realm I had not embraced prior to this occasion, ravens excepted (although I talk, or at least I mimic *their* language, they don't parrot back mine). True, I am a writer and writers do have rich imaginations. Regardless, until now the naturalist in me had avoided anthropomorphizing bears (like Winnie the Pooh), elephants (like Babar), or amphibians (like Mr. Toad of Toad Hall). Enough, already, with the talking pigs, talking mice, talking bunnies, talking spiders. I say, "Kill 'em all, Mr. McGregor, let God sort 'em out." Still, there's a first time for everything and hearing *is* believing. And this wild ragamuffin had spoken to me with real English words.

So I said, "I'm going to climb Spoon Mountain."

"Why?"

That was stretching it. What were we in for now, philosophical badinage about the meaning of human endeavor between an atheist intellectual and a famished brown bear? Should I give the silly answers of "Because it's there" or "To get to the other side?" A rank odor drifting off the weary animal contained an unpleasant mixture of sweat, infected saliva, garbage residue, and congealed blood. Flies buzzed around his body targeting in particular the mashed eye socket and a ring of dingleberries stuck to his butt hole. In daylight I could see that four of his six incisors were broken off, gone. A tongue emerged, licking snot off his gob. He hadn't a tenth of the glamour I'd noted during our nocturnal rumble on my kitchen stoop.

"I don't remember any more," I admitted. "I've lost the thread. But I haven't got a gun and I am not going to harm you."

The bear gave me what I can only call an ironic once-over. "You don't have a 'gun?'" he said. "And you're not going to 'harm' me?"

There followed a pause as we continued to confront each other. Behind the bear and to either side was the rugged basin whose western slope I had been climbing. I can't say that Scarface came across as a noble animal framed within a sublime high sierra landscape as if in a *Nova* documentary on PBS. He seemed puny and scabrous, more closely resembling a woodchuck that had been sideswiped by a Chevy Suburban while crossing I-25 than a ferocious and domineering predator. Old Ben he was not, nor, to be honest, could I remotely compare myself to Boon Hogganbeck. In my dreams. William Faulkner's purple prose and his Nobel Prize were safe from us.

So why was I tongue-tied with nothing more to say? I guess I felt foolish and embarrassed for being a human being. We should all be so contrite. Pride goeth before destruction, and a haughty spirit before a fall. Humility precedes renaissance. Then again, you can feel major-league foolish rapping in English with an English-speaking bear. The entire shtik doesn't sit right.

For the record, I believe I had a lot to say. I've never been to a psychiatrist, though, and could not imagine how to begin in this place with this sad animal as my father-confessor. You might infer that my entire life had been a prelude to, and a preparation for, this moment on the side of a mountain facing an undersized bear reduced to a Shadow of His Former Self by greenhouse gases and the luck of the draw. But that would be melodramatic and self-conscious. And even if true I had no idea how to rise to the occasion. In the movie version we would have wrestled to death on the side of Spoon Mountain and Scarface would have been a gigantic silver-haired grizzly even though the last grizzly from the Southwest was stabbed to death with a hunting arrow by an outfitter named Ed Wiseman in 1979 (cf. David Petersen, *Ghost Grizzlies* [Henry Holt and Company, New York, 1995]). Or, in another movie version, Scarface and I would inexplicably (and instantly) bond together and, after devouring a granola bar I gave to him, the bear would lead me up a mysterious secret trail to the summit of Spoon Mountain where we would sit side-by-side (perhaps paw in hand?) overlooking a vast digitized panorama where eagles soared beneath double rainbows while a fifty-piece symphony orchestra played the theme song from *Bonanza*.

In real life, bored, Scarface heaved to his feet and recommenced his upward toil skirting a widish path around me at a painful amble, mute as a mushroom. No threat was implied, no intentions of violence. Our interaction was over, minus all the kerfuffle this time around. We were both too pooped to pop. The bear was simply another listless creature with nothing left to lose and no higher purpose except survival until tomorrow, which would entail as little fraternization with the enemy as possible.

I watched him climb—pigeon-toed, neck bent, head hanging, mouth open—up the steep slope like the Little Engine that Could, one drab step at a time, inexorable, defeated, yet not dead yet. For an animal almost blind who must also have been drained he retained a remarkable focus on the goal ahead, never once swerving aside or pausing again to rest. He could have been the embodiment of my own fatigue walking away from me in the gruesome heat. How come nature refuses to cry "uncle"?

In due course he reached the ridgeline above, kept going, disappeared. At which point I'm afraid I totally lost my composure despite my repeated avowals not to. "Hey, let me explain!" I shouted at the Saddle. "Spoon Mountain is a symbol for all that we forfeited when agriculture changed the world and then industrial capital laid waste to the biology that sustains us while enslaving two-thirds of the earth's people in abject poverty and hopelessness! Spoon Mountain is a commitment to banish forever all our cruel economic, insane religious, and utterly banal philosophical beliefs while instituting social justice for all, an equal redistribution of wealth, ZPG, and an end to atomic bombs and nuclear power plants and growth for the sake of growth and racist violence against minorities. That commitment shall also include a declaration of ecoliberation for every animal, insect, bird, fish, reptile, tree, fungus, river, and marsupial around the globe, barring nobody and nothing from the manifesto, not even mosquitoes or ichneumon wasps or tomato hornworm caterpillars! *Power to the creatures!* Spoon Mountain insists that we reclaim the ecoimprinting which guides every other living molecular miracle in the great web of life except us, *homo sapiens*, who have abdicated from the genetic fundamentals that developed in us back during our hunter-gatherer days and could still save us if only we'd acknowledge them and act accordingly! It's as simple as that!"

There, I'd said it. Once again I had inserted my big foot into my big fat mouth, lock, stock and barrel. Blahdy blahdy blah blah blah.

Too late, however. Talk to a wall. By then hizzoner had plodded over to another alpine bowl where perhaps the going was . . . I won't say easier, because in nature nothing is easier. But maybe it would be different. And anyway, all the food available down in civilization wasn't worth the risk. For a bear there's always safety in a lack of numbers.

Thirty-nine

O nly two water bottles remained. Wincing from the effort, puzzled by my own delirious perseverance, I stood up, my joints grating audibly as I hobbled a final twenty yards to the Saddle, passing through the gap to a nubbin of shade where unexpected cold wind gusts flailed at my damp clothing causing a chill. I lost my balance and fell down and pushed upright again. Gasping, I gazed at the western panorama which included the Los Pinos watershed and Lake Fork Peak . . . and—oops!—many fierce flat-bottomed cumulonimbus clouds ranging in hue from very dark blue and purple to black suspended over the summit of Spoon Mountain barely a quarter mile above me.

No way.

To be charitable, I was astonished. *What kind of bad joke—?*

I inched around one degree at a time to face east of my position where not an errant puff of white marred the dirty azure expanse that had been overhead during my entire trip to the Saddle. The demarcation between drought, left, and pending tempest, right, was as sharp as a knife blade running from north to south along the ridge. Worse than exhausted, I whimpered, "Shucks." Not another challenge.

I was standing at 12,600 feet prepared to summit Spoon Mountain, a prosaic bump of no consequence except to a decrepit grandpa like me. A half mile to the south skeins of mist were already falling toward Cabrito Peak. The valley floor was blurred by haze below the thunderheads and I could not delineate Boulder Peak or Reliz Mesa fifty miles west near La Barranca. The Jemez Mountains were a faint silhouette through the smog.

I asked myself, "Do you think this is a life-threatening situation?"

Yes it was—*get out of here*—but I hesitated, calculating my chances of reaching the crest of Spoon Mountain alive. At this point a pragmatic person, a *cogent* human being, would have scrammed. I could retreat with honor, escaping blame, satisfied to have given it my best effort and nobody would call me a failure. Why not? Let Miranda explain:

"Because every year in the United States, Dad, a hundred and fifty irrational yo-yos are dispatched by lightning either while ambling across golf courses or hiking ridgetops above tree line. The brainpans of another two hundred 'survivors' are toasted for life by the bolts. So *go for it*."

"Yeah," Ben said, egging me on. "Knock yourself out, old man."

What to do? I had vowed to summit Spoon Mountain on my sixty-fifth birthday and I was within striking distance. I had labored so hard on this cockamamie excursion. And come on, get serious: *Not in this drought would it rain.* It couldn't rain. After months—years!—of watching the landscape shrivel and die moisture made no sense to me. And if I withdrew now would I regret that cowardly decision for the rest of my days? I was in a quandary.

Then I recalled a scene toward the conclusion of my novel *The Lucky Underdogs*, in which the main female character tells her hubby, my bumbling reluctant-hero chief protagonist, that all his life he's been waiting to do one great thing and now is his chance, so don't blow it. And, against all odds, he does not blow it. Somehow, despite his own fearfulness, and disregarding centuries of historical precedents stacked against him and his people of the valley, my timid protagonist musters the courage to perform an improbable and ridiculously valiant act that rescues his village from the depredations of a rapacious developer poised to transform its remote and picturesque setting into a ski area, resort hotel, and gambling casino complex that will embody every amoral value all rational people detest, and, during this process, the hardy indigenous culture that has persevered for centuries in that remote part of the southern Rockies will be destroyed. Instead, thanks to a heroic act by my protagonist, they are saved.

And so—?

Duly inspired, I realized the time had arrived to put my money where my mouth is. Life imitates art. "Those clouds are harmless," I said aloud. *"Let's do it."*

Forty

I bushwhacked through fellfields and sparse hair grasses toward the tantalizingly near summit, hunched over, pressed earthward by the weight of the cloudy sky. Between steps I leaned on my poles and counted to five, then forced another step, then counted to five anew. The air was heavy, not a current stirring, yet oxygen molecules crackled within the threatening ozone. Without trees or buildings to provide human-scale reference I was way overexposed and smaller than a freckle on the moon. I circled around an emaciated bee feeding at indigo-colored forget-me-nots. My body trembled, I had the shakes, I was so excited. *I'm almost there.*

"Just don't glance up," Miranda cautioned, "and try not to imagine what will happen if Mother Nature chooses to open her colossal maw and ingest you like a shark swallowing a mosquito."

"Or like a wolverine eating a white-footed deer mouse," Ben said gleefully.

"Quiet, you two. I'm *hiking*."

I tromped past a few innocent alpine daisies. There were sheep droppings but no bighorns visible anywhere.

Had they all evaporated in the drought? If only Ben and Miranda could be here now.

Where were they? Had Miranda and Michael and Lizzy driven back to the Capital City? How could they abandon me? (How could they not?) Why hadn't they talked me out of this? (Don't answer that question.) Whose children allowed their parents to commit suicide? (Whose parents were as deficient as me?) What about Jamie and Ben? I could understand Miranda's wrath, though not Ben's anger at Michael . . . and Jamie. Ben wasn't that kind of human being. Last night both Michael and Ben had defended me. Why? Or had they really? Would Michael and Miranda sue each other for divorce because of me? Would Lizzy wind up in an insane asylum for Raven speakers? Perhaps Jamie had called a lawyer this morning to obtain a restraining order against Ben for domestic violence. Now they'll never get hitched. It's all my fault. Poor Ben. Poor Jamie. She leads him around by a ring in his nose. She smothers him with her vicious kindness. All the same, he loves her. Why did he knock her into the refrigerator and then practically fracture her jaw? Is he currently cooling his heels in the same cell Don the Man recently vacated? What is love, anyway, a many-splendored thing? Or just another ball and chain? I wouldn't know, would I? My game has always been infatuation—pure ecstasy and then pure agony with nothing in between. The serial gigolo strikes again. "What's it all about, Alfie?" Roberto tells me, "Our Father gave little girls vaginas so little boys would talk to them." How can I persuade Sally to ignore my track record and try again? *I don't want to die alone.*

During another pause I noticed a cluster of what I believed were arctic gentians at my feet, delicate white tubes displaying thin lavender streaks on their sides. "According to my sources they bloom later in the summer," I explained to my kids. "Yet because of the drought these gentians must be emerging early—"

ZAP!!!!!!!!!!!!!!!!!!!

A ferocious electrical streak slashed from an anvil-shaped cumulonimbus formation smiting the top of Spoon Mountain and thunder boomed, which caused me to exclaim, *"Help!"* and then, *"Run for your life!"* And I finally abandoned ship and fled as marble-sized hail pelted my head and shoulders driven by a frenzied garble of wind and rain as lightning and another rumbleburst of thunder knocked me flat. *Here we go again.* CUE IN THEME MUSIC FOR TOM AND JERRY. Before I could push erect I was smashed back to earth by a huge gush of water spilling from the angry clouds. *Our Lord pisses from a very big dick!* Before I could catch my breath or don a poncho the temperature had dropped thirty degrees and I was drenched. Freezing and nearly hypothermal I raced down the steep pitch skidding on hail pellets, duck-waddling, crab-walking, lobster-scuttling belly-up on all fours while lightning lit the sizzling atmosphere and icy projectiles caromed off my body and jounced from the ground as wind smacked me over to my side, then forward onto my face, then back on my ass again and I lost my trekking poles.

Jesus! I cartwheeled into the shrubby cinquefoil bushes almost dislocating my left arm by grabbing branches as I careened past them in muddy goop and more hailstones, yelping at every electrical burst. The ground heaved up and clubbed me, my knapsack was torn off and bounced away, the sky spun around my head, I clutched at the earth as it roller-coastered past me too slippery to handle. Thunder and the clatter of raindrops and hail were totally unnerving as I plummeted downhill at the mercy of the berserk elements . . . and by the time I landed at the boulder pile two hundred feet below I had wrenched my left knee and both ankles, banged my broken arm many times, lacerated several fingers, and uttered numerous panicked blasphemies. There was no letup from the loud detonations and countless volts of electricity going ape, the convulsions of turbulent air. *"A Don the Man the size of God is attacking me!"* My hair was plastered across my forehead and rain torrents poured off my nose and down my neck as the hail bombardment intensified. When had anyone ever been so manhandled by the weather? *"Ben and Miranda were right, I'm a fool, I deserve to croak!"* But I kept moving because not to move was not an option. Desperate to reach the shelter of tree line I staggered forward avoiding boulders that wallowed across my path, drunken and dangerous. My calves were on fire; both shoulders felt separated. Water splattered against those shoulders driven hard by furious blasts of air and another lightning bolt was hurled at me for breaking the law on a mountaintop.

I fell, bashing my knee. *"Ouch!"* Clouted into submission I hunkered beside a large stone expecting a heart attack, wheezing from asthma as I strained to see through the ice balls, the deafening cannonade of rain and lightning. *Oh what a wet world it was dumbstruck by inundation!* And when thunder again clapped directly overhead I pissed in my britches discharging the urine so emphatically I thought it *was* the heart attack. I clasped my hands over my head expecting that the next barrage would annihilate me leaving only a small puddle of excrement, a fiberglass arm cast, an aluminum pinkie splint, and miscellaneous gory organ bits on the stone beneath my feet.

Instead—gunshot sudden—a miracle took place. The hail ceased, slamming on its brakes inches in front of me and the rain also quit, thunder muttered once more only half as threatening and then evaporated, the lightning ended—*zip!*—and a final wave of icy water mixed with graupel sloshed against my feet as it drained into the boulders and disappeared leaving behind a truly fantastic silence. "Oh my goodness." It had been six minutes of deluge, start to finish, almost as fast as whiplash. I cringed, awaiting the next onslaught, but the storm had stopped . . . short . . . never to go again. Icy wind swirled around my damp body setting my teeth achatter. All the parts of my exposed flesh that weren't muddy had turned cobalt blue.

A thousand clouds evaporated justlikethat revealing an unblemished sky so benign it was inane. Warm sunlight fell upon heaven and earth. Across the way the highest third of Gavilán Peak was brightly silvered by hail and the entire basin gleamed with spectacular brilliance, trees steaming, cliffs shimmering. A pika chirped. And a dozen curious pipits alighted on the nearby rocks, bobbing their narrow tails.

Amazing. I was still alive. I could not breathe, however, and my inhaler was in the knapsack up higher on the mountain. My water was in the knapsack, also. My jacket was in the knapsack. Sadly, I could not move. My heart had gone completely haywire, a bucking bronco. I did the Valsalva maneuver, straining abdominal muscles downward which didn't work. I tried it again to no avail. When I took a deep breath and held it and strained as if constipated the procedure was totally ineffective. My racing ticker flip-flopped out of control. A heart in such disarray dehydrates you exponentially, but I had no water to drink.

"Oh dear."

Forty-one

To be fair, I will now describe the summit of Spoon Mountain. I owe my readers that. After all, I had reached the top often during my younger days, my children did also.

Miranda and I always shouted, "Look at the splendor around us!" Ben smiled. Eastward, a mile across the Gallegos Lake basin, stood Gavilán Peak. To the immediate left steep scree slides and near vertical cliffs led down to Spoon Mountain's north cirque. Directly in front, over a thin buttress ridge, talus fans flanking a narrow grassy draw fell deep into the south cirque past a small tarn surrounded by more bulky rubble of stones. Lower still, cushioning the bottom third of the basin, was the Engelmann spruce forest descending to Gallegos Lake.

Around to the west, directly off the Spoon summit, the drop was sharp to massive disorderly rock piles bleeding into heavily forested Deer Creek Canyon under South Fork Peak.

We could see well over a hundred miles southward to Durazno Peak, a soft gray hump rising above the Capital City where my daughter, her husband, and Lizzy now dwell. En route our eyes brushed over many dramatic summits of the Coyote Peaks in the Rio Blanco wilderness. Far to their right the Jemez chain of mountains ran about fifty miles west of Spoon Mountain. When we turned around facing north even larger mountains rambled forty miles up to the Colorado border and beyond to Blanca Mountain and the twin Spanish Peaks.

We were standing on a patch of gravel and short grass beside a shambles of scoured boulders with unobstructed space expanding in all directions. No plant grew higher than the Swoosh marks on our sneakers. A pair of strange white butterflies fluttered by inches above the fellfield. They were called parnassians, and you might even see them flying in a snowstorm.

Off the summit, seventy yards south on Spoon Ridge at the same height, was Catherine Lake Overlook. On the way there we trudged past yellow alpine avens in patches of low tundra grasses surrounded by peach-colored rocks. There were bright alpine primroses the size of my thumbnail and cushions of miniature rockjasmines, also delicate sandwort flowers floating barely above the ground. Nonstop wind and year-round snows and constant solar radiation had leveled everything. Whatever was alive hugged the earth, straining to survive. A plant no bigger than a nickel might be thirty years old.

We followed a narrow bighorn sheep trail that ran along the spine of the ridge past a few alpine sunflowers five inches tall: Old Men of the Mountain they are called. A one-ounce chipmunk flicked its tail and vanished among the talus where small piles of drying grasses on flat slabs had been assembled by pikas for their winter food supply.

Winding dirt eskers from pocket gophers lay underfoot; pale green lichens stretched across metamorphic stone. Most of the remaining turf was swept clean but for pebbles, gravel, sand, bits of shattered granite, and dust scuffed in swirls from wind abrading the dry surfaces.

We stopped and gazed down at Catherine Lake four hundred feet under the overlook in another cirque. Talus and boulder deposits gave way near the shoreline to dwarf junipers and veins of arctic willows and bristlecone pines. Helter-skelter rocky debris rose east of the lake up to the craggy top of Cabrito Peak. There, a half-dozen bighorn rams kept watch over their domain. They looked so *proud*. Exiting Catherine Lake a no-name creek trickled through a narrow gap into Oso Canyon.

The wind stung our cheeks and snot splashed against our faces. Tears dribbled from the corners of our eyes. Our jackets puffed out, filled with attacking air. We were near an island of yellow avens with black-tipped sedge growing among them. Wind flattened the vegetation into silvery hues. Small bees and butterflies searched for nectar along the ground, flying under the wind. Everywhere the landscape was empty but not empty. It was enormous. The air sparkled. The views were lucid. Our feet wanted to release the earth so we could tumble into the sky. We were besotted with clichés. That euphoria happens at altitude when you are dazzled by a piece of geography untrammeled by human ingenuity.

I skirt sierras, my palms cover continents, I am afoot with my vision. Walt Whitman wrote those words.

I remember sitting on that spot with Ben and Miranda

glassing a band of fifteen cow elk with their calves bedded around Catherine Lake below. The blue sky held a few tranquil clouds. It was a moment of windless relaxation we rarely experienced that high. All three of us were peering down at the elk through our binoculars. The animals seemed placid, at rest, and not especially alert as they baked in their oval of warmth.

"I won't ever forget this," Miranda vowed.

"Me neither," Ben said.

Miranda lowered her binoculars. "Dad, promise me you'll bring us up here every year at least once, the three of us together, until death do us part."

"I promise," I said.

"Are your fingers crossed?"

"No." I showed her my hands, palms up, fingers spread wide.

"Ben, do you promise to always come along with us during this ritual no matter what?"

Ben nodded his head.

"Say it out loud," Miranda insisted.

"I promise," Ben said.

Miranda switched back to me. "Do you swear on a stack of Bibles?"

"'Bibles?'" I asked, frowning.

"I'm speaking metaphorically, Dad. Don't be obtuse. You're old enough to know better."

"Okay," I said. "I swear."

"You're not lying? Because lying is not acceptable on this one. You have to be telling the truth for once."

"I'm telling the truth," I said. "I promise."

Miranda was relieved. "Okay. I'm glad that's settled. I really like it up here with you and Ben." She raised her binoculars to check out the elk some more. A merlin zipped past us and dived toward Catherine Lake, gone in an instant. We were at peace and contented together, close to our own true ecology. Our hearts belonged to nature and therefore we belonged to each other.

The world held its breath.

Eight months later I married Tammy Pierce and Miranda went to war with her. Ben quickly abdicated what he did not understand. Then I was sidetracked for years with Hollywood, heart problems, another marriage and divorce, and many other distractions, and my kids were distracted also. We three never climbed Spoon Mountain again. We never camped again at Gallegos Lake, either. You would not believe how fast things can fall apart when promises are broken. I lost touch with my own children. I lost touch with the *earth*. And the years whizzed by like rooftops blown off by a hurricane.

Forty-two

"**O**kay," Miranda said. "Shake a leg you old fuddy-duddy. You think you're immortal but you're not. Under the right circumstances it's really easy for people to die."

"I don't want to scatter your ashes," Ben said. "You're not going to die."

Miranda said, "Just because you've dodged so many bullets in the past doesn't mean the next one doesn't have your name on it."

Ben said, "We're not disrespecting you, Pop, we care about you."

And Miranda said, "We don't want to lose you yet."

Voices. I was hearing their voices in my pipe dreams.

Miranda was a tall girl with intense green eyes that always twinkled and a raucous comical manner. She was a fine nurse, a good mother, a loving wife . . . and my gracious daughter. Ben was six-two, he weighed two-ten, he had a square jaw and a crew cut. Every three days he programmed an insulin pump to save his life. When he was born he never made a sound, he started looking around as if he could actually see things that nobody else could fathom.

But I had broken our frail bonds last night. I was so tired I could not stand up. I was wheezing, gulping for air, painfully thirsty. My heart had quieted, remaining irregular, leaving me muddleheaded and nauseated. I had given up on the Valsalva maneuver. The sun dropped behind Spoon Ridge. Frigid shadows took over my east-facing slope. The hail had melted off the top third of Gavilán Peak across the basin where sunlight still reined. Maybe the drought was over, at least for now. Spoon Mountain would remain unconquered on my sixty-fifth birthday, however. I had come close but no cigar. "That's okay," Miranda said. "Maybe tomorrow. After all, tomorrow is another day."

No, tomorrow would not be another day.

I scanned the lower slopes one last time to see if my offspring were climbing up to save their dad. No, they were nowhere in sight. Serves me right. You get what you pay for. I was cold and wet and shivering. My body felt as if it had been maimed in my eighth car accident. And then I saw them, only a quarter mile below, trudging along and aiming in my direction. Really? My heart stopped . . . and began again, *finally*, in sinus rhythm. I rubbed my good eye and refocused the binoculars. Really. Miranda and Ben were ascending the mountain toward me. Incredible. They were not a hallucination. They were breaking the law, violating the hiking ban due to fire danger. *Ben* was breaking the law. For me. Or maybe for himself? With my glasses trained on him I waved until finally he glanced up and saw me and waved back at me. Miranda was following right behind him. She looked up and also waved. She *waved*.

They did not stop. They were proceeding at a steady

clip because time was running out. This side of the basin was dark and growing colder. Night comes fast to the mountains. Miranda had on khaki shorts and her Gore-Tex hiking boots and a baseball cap and a knapsack. She was using poles. Ben wore a T-shirt and Wrangler jeans and his Red Wing boots. His fat backpack probably held the oxygen tank and the defibrillator kit. He had no hiking sticks. Ben is a mule, as I used to be. He could carry Miranda and all their equipment uphill if he had to. Ben is strong. You look at him you think Paul Bunyan, you think John Henry. Ben could break your ribs by accident if (by accident) he embraced you. Ben does not know his own strength.

Intending to rise and limp downhill toward them I took a final glimpse around at the mountains and rock piles and the clear sky. But I could not get to my feet. My legs refused to cooperate. I was numb and light-headed from asthma. My throat was way too dry. I was freezing cold. You can imagine how I felt, or maybe you can't. I felt almost blissful and also horribly chagrined. I had gotten my comeuppance. I felt helpless and grateful. I felt like a kid who has thrown a ridiculous tantrum and knows it and they were coming for me anyway. I was a boy who had cried "Wolf!" once too often and yet survived the attack. When they reached me I would apologize for last night. Hat in hand, I would apologize for many things. We live in a world of grief during an age of grief and I have done my unruly part to bring grief upon myself and others. Yet our obligation is to keep rising from the ashes.

So I prepared myself to meet the children, hoping they'd welcome me back from my long exile. Of course, whatever imaginary credibility I might have thought I possessed with them was gone. It had been absent since they were youngsters, who did I think I was kidding? And why should they welcome me back? What had I ever done to merit that? Maybe they'd only hiked this high to bid me farewell in person. A point of honor. Then they would about-face and hightail it to safety, leaving me adrift. "See you around the campus, Dad. Rot in Hades."

As they drew closer I grew woozy from apprehension. *Here it comes*, I thought. *My just desserts. Steel yourself.*

"Hello, we're here," Miranda said, taking off her knapsack. She knelt in front of me and placed her hand upon my knee. "Gosh," she said, "you look awful." And Ben? Ben did not say a word. He removed a fleece jacket from his backpack and draped it over my shoulders. Then he unscrewed the cap off a water bottle and passed me the bottle. Next, out came the oxygen canister.

"I'm really sorry," I said. "I apologize for last night. I apologize for everything."

Miranda said, "Well, it's about time you apologized, Papa-san. And we forgive you. But you owe us eight million dollars in reparations at thirteen percent annual interest for the past three decades of neglect. Did you reach the top?"

"No. However, I came close."

"Close only counts in horseshoes, old man. Better luck next time."

"We're sorry too," Ben said. And he meant it. He had not turned into a werewolf becoming Ben the Barbarian. As far as I could tell he was the same shy and gentle overgrown boy I had known all my life. The other all-new Ben had been a typical figment of my hysterical imagination. I should have tendered him way more credit.

Miranda gave me an inhaler. I took two puffs and immediately could breathe again, thank Christ. I drank half the water bottle's contents in three swallows and finished the job in three more. Ben unscrewed the cap of another bottle and handed it over and I polished off the entire thing without lowering the mouth from my lips. Miranda clicked open her First Aid kit and swabbed my bloody fingers with an alcohol wipe and bandaged them while Ben watched. The pinkie splint had survived. She dabbed the blood off my face careful not to bump against my aching nose.

"You *truly* look awful," she said.

"What happened in my kitchen last night?" I asked.

Ben averted my eyes.

Miranda said, "We had a family discussion, no big deal. Don't get in a twit. Michael had a fantasy he wears the pants, but that's over now. And you'll survive."

"What about Jamie?"

"She's happy. Ben finally sucked it up and asked her to marry him. Right, Ben?"

Ben made a slight hand gesture.

"What about Lizzy?"

"You're still the cat's pajamas in her book. Kids are resilient. Also, we bribed her by promising to buy her a cell phone. And it's all because of you. So now she thinks you're double God. Relax and count your blessings. Every lining has a silver cloud."

I said, "I had a terrible nightmare about Don the Man. He came to my house with his baseball bat and I shot him."

"Not to worry," Miranda said. "Didn't you hear on the radio this morning? Your nemesis is in Holy Cross Hospital with a shoulder wound because some wacko sheriff's deputy caught him last night in flagrante delicto with his wife, who's a local magistrate judge. An anonymous tipster was involved. A half-naked Catholic priest who inexplicably jumped out of her closet coldcocked the gun-toting deputy and then called 911 because *he* had a heart attack himself."

I absorbed that for a moment. "For reals?"

"You can take it to the bank. And one other thing," Miranda said. "As Michael and Lizzy and I were packing around noon today your girlfriend arrived at the hotel and insisted we come search for you here. She was adamant. I liked her."

"Sally is my ex-girlfriend," I said.

"That's not the impression I got. Do you want a hit of oxygen before we start downhill?"

"I don't need no stinking oxygen," I said.

Nodding, she closed her First Aid kit and stashed it in her knapsack. "Alley oop oop, then. Time's a wasting. It's late. We better hustle what's left of you out of here." She adjusted her trekking poles for my height and handed them over. "What happened to your sticks and other stuff?"

"I lost them in the storm."

Ben reached down, grasping my hand, and pulled me to my feet. I wobbled for a second, feeling sick and dizzy. When things cleared a bit I took a step or two, gingerly. My heart lurched.

I said, "Thank you for these trekking poles, Miranda."

"You're welcome."

She gave me a hug. Then she stepped aside and told Ben, "Go ahead."

"Go ahead, what?"

"*Hug* him."

Ben hugged me.

I said, "Will you guys come back up here with me if I try again?"

"Sure," Miranda said, "if you get into shape for two months, follow a diet and lose twenty pounds then we'll talk turkey after you do a treadmill that says you're game to go, fair enough?"

"Yes," I said. "I guess."

"You 'guess?'"

"No, I accept your terms," I mumbled contritely. That wasn't easy.

A movement caught my eye. Two ravens had appeared overhead doing a dance. They zoomed and twisted side by side through the cleansed atmosphere, then spiraled earthward and zigzagged together only inches apart, perfectly synchronized like a pair of Olympic figure skaters except much swifter. A wild fey exuberance highlighted their shenanigans. They were unfettered and beautiful. With a flutter they looped upward again until they stalled and tumbled end over end toward the ground once more in free fall, their wingtips and talons touching until they bottomed out and swooped west gliding quickly over the top of Spoon Mountain out of sight—*adiós!*—leaving the air behind them immaculate.

And I?

I was about to call after the birds when Miranda beat

me to the punch, giving three loud quorks that sounded as perfect as if she had learned them right off the Raven CD I sent to Lizzy. I could not have done better myself.

Miranda then winked at me, saying, "Bueno. Chop chop, Dad. Move it or lose it. Get the lead out." Shadows were rising fast up the west face of Gavilán Peak.

"Okay, I'm ready," I said.

My daughter replied, "I hope so."

And Ben said, "Don't be a turtle, be a rabbit."